# ASHLEY LITTLE

ARSENAL PULP
PRESS
VANCOUVER

NIAGARA MOTEL
Copyright © 2016 by Ashley Little

ARSENAL PULP PRESS
Suite 202 – 211 East Georgia St.
Vancouver, BC V6A 1Z6
Canada
*arsenalpulp.com*

The publisher gratefully acknowledges the support of the Canada Council for the Arts and the British Columbia Arts Council for its publishing program, and the Government of Canada (through the Canada Book Fund) and the Government of British Columbia (through the Book Publishing Tax Credit Program) for its publishing activities.

This is a work of fiction. Any resemblance of characters to persons either living or deceased is purely coincidental.

Cover and text design by Oliver McPartlin
Edited by Susan Safyan

Printed and bound in Canada

Library and Archives Canada Cataloguing in Publication:
Little, Ashley, 1983-, author
     Niagara motel / Ashley Little.

Issued in print and electronic formats.
ISBN 978-1-55152-660-7 (paperback).—ISBN 978-1-55152-661-4 (html)


     I. Title.

PS8623 I898 N53 2016          C813'.6          C2016-904377-0
                                               C2016-904378-9

For Warren

# PART ONE

# THE MOTEL LIFE

# 1

I was born in a laundromat in Paris, Ontario. If you knew Gina you wouldn't think it was that weird. Gina is my mother. She says she's a dancer. What that means is she's a stripper. Sometimes she says exotic dancer if she's really comfortable with you. Sometimes she goes all the way and there's another word for that. But I'm not allowed to say it. Not when Gina's around. Sometimes late at night when Gina's at work and I can't sleep and I'm lying in bed in whatever crap-hat motel room we're in, I whisper it up to the ceiling, *whore, hoo-er, hoaaar*. And sometimes I think that word sounds kind of beautiful.

Gina has a condition. It's not her fault. She had it before me and it got worse after she had me. It's called narcolepsy with cataplexy. The doctors took a long time to figure out what was wrong with her. Some people thought she was lazy, some people thought she was severely depressed, some people thought she was a drug addict, but Gina's not any of those things. What happens is she falls asleep a lot. Then other times, she gets a sleep attack where she conks out and can't move, but she's not *actually* asleep, she can still see and hear. That's the cataplexy part. Sometimes she falls asleep while driving and that's how I learned to drive when I was seven and why we mostly take the bus now. Sometimes she falls asleep when we're walking down the sidewalk, and I have to stay beside her and make sure nobody steals her purse. Sometimes she falls asleep when she's at work but the managers don't know about narcolepsy with cataplexy and they think Gina's messed up on drugs so she gets fired and then we have to get our skinny asses the heck out of Dodge, as Gina says. Other things happen to Gina too because of the narcolepsy. She can't sleep at night like regular people do. She sometimes has dreams *while* she's awake and when she has nightmares, she thinks they're really happening. She has medicine for it but it's really expensive and it doesn't always work and sometimes she runs out and doesn't get more for a while. The medicine is called GHB which is the same thing that's in the date rape drug. I've heard Gina tell her friends that she's the only person she knows who gives *herself* roofies, and then they all bust a gut laughing like it's the funniest thing in the world.

I'm eleven years old and I've been to sixteen different schools. Last summer we rode the Greyhound from Penetanguishene to Prince George and stopped in all the dumb little towns along the way so Gina could work. Gina says I've seen more of the country than most adults.

It's not so bad, I guess. Sometimes if I start making friends with kids at school, or if I can tell a girl has a crush on me or something, I'll wish we didn't have to leave so soon, but sometimes if I don't like my teacher or the kids are mean, then I'm glad we get to leave, so it's good but it's bad too. Mostly, I keep to myself and read books at lunch and recess. I used to figure, what's the point of making friends since we're just going to leave in a few months anyways? But recently, I realized that even if you have a friend for one week or one month, and you're super sad when you have to leave them, it's worth it.

\*\*\*

So one night I'm sitting around in my underwear in our room at the Prince Motel, eating salt and vinegar chips, watching *Late Night with David Letterman*, and Gina comes in, looking tired 'cause she always looks tired, 'cause she doesn't sleep properly on account of her condition.

"Hey, Tucker."

"Hey. How come you're home so early?"

She sat down on the bed and took a chip out of the bag and ate it. Then she took another one. "How do you feel about Niagara Falls?"

"I don't know. Have I been there before?" I kept watching *Letterman*, but I could see out of the corner of my eye that she was looking at me with that mushy face she sometimes gets when she's sad.

"No, you haven't."

I shrugged. "Okay."

Gina figures there are more people in Ontario so there's more married businessmen there and married businessmen are the best tippers. Also, a woman named Daisy that she worked with in Edmonton told her that Niagara Falls was a goldmine. So the next morning we packed up all our stuff then went for breakfast at Denny's. I got the Lumberjack Slam and Gina got what she always gets, the Moons Over My Hammy because she loves saying it and thinks it's hilarious.

"Give me a sip of your chocolate milk."

I slid my glass over to her.

"Do you want a bite of my Moons Over My Hammy?" She started to laugh. Then it happened.

Her head hit the side of the plate as she slumped over the table. Her eyes were open and she was looking at me, sort of, but she was totally paralyzed. The waiter came over, flapping his arms around like a startled pigeon.

"Oh my God! Is she okay? Do you want me to call 9-1-1?"

"No. Don't worry." I reached across the table for the ketchup and squirted a pile of it onto my plate. "This happens all the time."

He stared at Gina and looked like he might start to cry.

"Do you have any hot sauce?"

# 2

The Greyhound bus from Prince George, BC, to Niagara Falls, Ontario, takes three days, eight hours, and fifteen minutes. Gina wanted to get there as soon as possible, and since we didn't have to stay in a motel for three nights, we'd have a little extra money so we could do some fun stuff like go to Marineland and Ripley's Believe It or Not! and crap like that.

Gina slept for the entire trip. I didn't even see her get up to go to the bathroom. I tried to wake her up a few times when we'd stop for meal breaks but she'd just turn toward the window and scrunch up more in her seat. I remember she told me once that the only time she can get a really good sleep is when she's riding in a car or on a bus. Something about the motion of the road being like a cradle, rocking her to sleep.

The woman across the aisle from us had curly blonde hair, enormous boobs, and a leopard-print shirt. She did crossword puzzles, drank Diet Coke, and smoked one cigarette every time we stopped. She kept her cigarettes in a little silver case. I think they were menthols but I couldn't be sure. The first night on the bus, she was sleeping and her blouse kind of fell open and I could see a little bit of her nipple. I stared at it for about two hours until I fell asleep.

The next morning we were somewhere in the mountains and she smiled at me. Her lips were all glistening and pink.

"Do you want a piece of gum?" She held out a stick of Juicy Fruit across the aisle.

"Sure." I took it and our fingers touched. "Thanks."

"That your mom?"

"Yeah."

"What's she do?"

"You mean besides sleep?"

She laughed. "Yeah."

I looked at the woman clacking her fake nails against the arm rest. I shrugged. "Same as you, I guess."

She sniffed. "Oh yeah, what's that?"

"She's a washed-up touring stripper."

She blinked a few times, and I could see the globs of mascara flaking off around her eyes, then she turned toward the window. The next time the bus stopped, she moved all her stuff up to the front, and I didn't see her or her nipples for the rest of the trip.

When I was younger, Gina would sometimes bring home friends from work after her shift. They would drink wine coolers and eat pistachios and laugh and tell jokes that I didn't understand the punch lines to. They told me that I was adorable and I used to love them all. With their high, tight boots and their colourful sparkly bras, I thought they looked like superheroes. But eventually, they all started to look the same, and somehow, as I got older, they got older too. Their laughs got raspier and their makeup got thicker, and instead of telling jokes, they complained about everything in the world. They stopped telling me I was adorable and started telling me to treat women right and never to break anyone's heart, to put the toilet seat down and stand up straight, to wear a condom, but if I forgot, at least stick around if I ever got a girl pregnant, and to always, always, *always* leave a tip for good service. Roz always gave me these pointers while pinching my cheeks. Roz was Gina's friend who didn't have any skin between her nostrils, just one giant nostril, and looking at her was like staring into a black hole. Roz pinched my cheeks so hard sometimes I had to go to school the next day with two blue bruises on my face. One day I told Gina I was sick of her friends telling me what to do all the time and just who did they think they were anyways?

"They're my friends, Tucker," she said. "They just want the best for you."

"They're stupid."

"Don't say that."

"Why not? It's true."

She sighed. "It might be true, but everyone needs friends. Especially when they don't have a family."

"I'm your family," I said.

"Yes, you are."

"Isn't that enough?"

"Look," Gina said. "What if I told you that you couldn't hang out with your friends? How would you like that?"

I shrugged. "I wouldn't care."

"You wouldn't care?"

"We're never in one place long enough for me to make friends anyways so it doesn't even matter," I said.

"You've had friends before," Gina said.

"Not really."

She looked at me and tilted her head to the side.

"I've never had a *best* friend."

Her eyes got misty. She touched my hair but I pulled away. "One day we'll find a place that's just right and stay there for a good long while," she said.

"Like a whole year?"

"At least a year, maybe more."

"Okay," I said. "That would be good."

She smiled.

"But can you tell Roz not to pinch my cheeks anymore? I really hate it."

"I can do that," she said.

When I saw Roz after that, she didn't pinch my cheeks, but she gave me noogies, which hurt even worse, but at least didn't leave bruises.

\*\*\*

I put my seat back and slept for awhile. I woke up sometime in the middle of the night to a car horn beeping and couldn't get back to sleep. I read my book, *Choose Your Own Adventure: The Abominable Snowman*. I got to climb Mount Everest but I kept dying. Once I was swallowed by an avalanche. Once I went too high up the mountain without letting myself acclimatize to the lack of oxygen. The third time, I froze to death because I lent my jacket to a friend who had fallen on a patch of ice and broken his arm. I didn't want to die anymore and I didn't care about finding the stupid Yeti either. He probably didn't even exist. Why do some people spend their entire lives hunting for creatures that no one really believes are real anyways? Why doesn't anyone take them by the shoulders and yell in their face, "Hey! Look! This thing you've spent your *whole life* thinking about and looking for doesn't friggin' *exist* so you can stop wasting your time now and go do something *useful!*" I shoved the book to the bottom of my backpack. There was another book in there that Mrs Jamieson, the librarian at my school in Prince George, had given me on my last day, *Where the Red Fern Grows*. It had a big stamp across the top that said DISCARDED. I spent the rest of the night reading it. Then I was glad that leopard-shirt lady had moved up front and Gina was zonked out, because I got kind of emotional over that book, and I didn't want either of them to see me like that. I stared out the window at the sunrise. It looked like someone had spilled their orange juice across the prairie sky. I wondered what it would be like to have a dog, to have anyone love you so much that they would sacrifice their own life for yours. I looked over at Gina. She was fast asleep. Her white-blonde hair fell around her face like dandelion fluff. I thought about how she'd had me when she was just a teenager, practically still a kid, like me—and that maybe, in a way, she had done that for me. Then I thought about how if Gina died, I would probably stop eating too, like little Ann had done when Old Dan died. And as I drifted off to sleep, I hoped that when Gina and I were dead and gone, someone would plant a red fern between our gravestones.

*** 

We picked a motel that was away from the strip because Gina said it would be quieter. What she meant was, it would be cheaper. The paint on the sign out front was all cracked and peeling so you could barely read what it said. If you stood back and squinted you could almost make the letters out. It said, Niagara Motel. I thought it sounded regal. When we passed the payphone in the lobby I imagined calling up Bryce, a boy I knew from Prince George, and telling him that I was glad to finally be out of stinky P.G. and that I was staying at the Niagara Motel. And that my life was absolutely wonderful and would be from now on.

I was excited to be in a new city, but most of all, I was happy to be off the bus. My back hurt and my feet felt fat and my mouth was all dried up inside. Gina, on the other hand, had just broken the Guinness World Record for Longest Nap Ever Taken and was practically glowing from the rejuvenation of it all. After we checked into our room and had showers, we got Cool Ranch Doritos and Crystal Pepsi from the vending machine. Gina said Crystal Pepsi was better for us because it was clear and that it tasted the exact same as regular Pepsi. Not very often, but sometimes Gina is *very* wrong about things.

How could a clear drink taste the same as a coloured drink? It was pretty much impossible. I hated Crystal Pepsi but drank it anyways because I was so thirsty. Then we went out to explore our new town. Gina and I went to a wax museum, and Brick City where you could build stuff with LEGO all day, and even though I'm way too old for LEGO now, it was still pretty cool. The wax museum was my favourite though. Upstairs it was all wax movie stars like Marilyn Monroe and the Terminator and that president of the United States who was also an actor, but downstairs was called The House of Horrors and it had all these famous criminals from the olden days. There was lots of blood and guts and gross write-ups about what the criminals had done and how many people they had killed and Gina said it wasn't appropriate but she let me look at it all anyways because I said it was a history lesson, and besides that, we had already paid.

"How come criminals get to be as famous as movie stars, even though they do bad things?" I asked as we studied the wax figure of Jack the Ripper.

"I don't know," Gina said. "I guess you don't need to have any real talent to become famous." She put her hand on my arm. "Let's get out of here. This place gives me the creeps."

We went to an IMAX and learned all about the legend of the Maid of the Mist and the people who went over the falls in barrels and survived, then we got mini-donuts and hot chocolate and rode the Ferris wheel for about an hour. We were supposed to get off after the wheel went around three times, but Gina blew a kiss to the operator and he let us stay on. When we finally got off he asked Gina for her number. She said we didn't have one yet because we just moved here, which was true.

"Maybe I can take you out for coffee sometime, then." He looked down at his boots, then back up at her.

"Oh, I don't drink coffee. Can't sleep if I drink it."

This was also true. But it was kind of sad how his face fell as she said it. She grabbed my hand then and pulled me away. "Thanks for the ride!"

I jerked my hand back and shoved it in my pocket and looked around to make sure no one had seen me holding hands with my mom. Gina laughed at me but I didn't care. I had to start school here soon and she didn't. I stopped to re-tie my shoe. Gina put her hair back in a ponytail so it wouldn't obstruct her view of the falls.

We walked along the boardwalk and gawked at the falls with everybody else. A family of Japanese tourists asked Gina to take their picture and she made them do all these crazy poses and had everyone cracking up. Then she turned the camera on herself and gave it the thumbs-up while she took a photo. This put them into hysterics.

I liked Niagara Falls right away because the people we saw kind of looked like us, like they didn't quite know what they were doing, but they were going to try to have a good time anyways.

*** 

The next day, we had breakfast at the Horton's across the street. Gina read the paper and I dug a hole through my muffin so that it became a duffin. Or a mo-nut. It was my own invention and one day I would sell the idea to Mr Horton for a gazillion dollars. Gina circled an ad in the classifieds and I leaned over to read what it said.

"Orchid Industries Escort Services. That sounds kind of nice."

Gina looked up from the paper. "Do you know what an escort is, Tucker?"

"Sure. It's like a Taurus but boxier."

She smiled. "Yeah, that's a Ford Escort. This is a different kind of escort."

"What kind?"

She popped a Timbit into her mouth. "It's like a date."

"Don't talk with your mouth full—jeez, you know that grosses me out."

"Sorry," she said, and covered her mouth. She swallowed, took a sip of her tea. "It's like a date."

"Oh."

"It's very classy. Only really classy ladies can do it."

"Guess you're S.O.L. then, hey?"

She rolled up the paper and swatted me on the arm with it while I laughed and choked a little bit on my duffin.

She unrolled the paper. "Want your horoscope?"

"Sure."

"Virgo, Virgo. There you are. All right." She cleared her throat. "Even if you don't have the faintest idea what is going on around you at the moment, act as if you have seen it all before. Create the illusion that you are in control. It's remarkable how easily most people are fooled."

"Lame. What's yours?"

"You may be in the minority as far as certain viewpoints are concerned but according to the planets you are on the side of the angels, so stop worrying about what others might think and do what you know to be right."

"So what are we doing today?"

"Well, I need to find a job, for one."

"I think what you meant to say was, we're going to Marineland."

"Ha-ha."

"I'm serious. We need to see the whales. Do what you know to be right, Gina."

"Do you like to eat?"

"Yeah."

"Do you like to wear clothes?"

"Uh ... I guess."

"Then I need to work."

"Work schmerk."

"Tucker—"

"But you *promised*."

She shook her head and started reading the paper again.

"Killer whales, Gina. Baby belugas. Sea lions!" I clapped my palms together, "Arf! Arf! Arf!"

"Shh! You're gonna get us kicked out of here."

"ARF! ARF! ARF!"

"Okay, I'll make you a deal. I'll look for work today and we'll go to Marineland tomorrow."

"No deal."

"Hey. Who's the boss?"

"Bruce Springsteen."

"You little sh—"

"Fifty bucks."

"Fifty bucks what?"

"Give me fifty bucks and you've got a deal."

Her mouth twisted up but her eyes were shining. "Twenty."

"Forty-five. That's as low as I'll go."

She took two twenties out of her wallet and shoved them at me. "Don't spend it all on candy."

We went back to our motel so Gina could get ready. I watched *The Simpsons* and thought about what I would do with my forty bucks. I could take a cab out to Marineland and see the whales myself, but it wouldn't be as much fun without Gina there. I could go on the Maid of the Mist and get soaking wet, but what's the point of getting soaking wet when there's no one around to laugh with? She came out of the bathroom then, big hair, short skirt, makeup, the shoes.

"How do I look?"

I shrugged.

She pushed her boobs up and checked herself out in the mirror above the desk. "This is big, Tucker. This is Niagara-fuckin-Falls."

"When will you be back?"

"I don't know. I'll call you."

"What if I'm not here?"

"Then I'll leave a message on the motel phone."

"Okay. Well, break a leg."

"Thanks, lamb chop." She kissed me on the forehead and grabbed her purse. "Don't forget to eat lunch."

"Don't forget to eat dinner."

"Don't forget to brush your teeth."

"Don't forget to wipe your butt."

"Don't forget I love you."

"Don't forget to close the door behind you."

She blew me a kiss and left.

\*\*\*

I wandered up and down Clifton Hill for most of the day. I saw some guys smoking out of a glass tube in an alley behind the 7-Eleven. I saw a fat man yelling into a payphone about losing everything he owned. I watched a black-haired girl in a too-tight dress pose on the corner and lean into car windows. I thought about going back to Brick City to build more stuff with LEGO, but I like to try new things so I went to the arcade instead. I saw some kids I thought maybe I could be friends with but then I saw them snickering when I was playing Ms. Pac-Man, even though I'm pretty good at Ms. Pac-Man and Ms. Pac-Man is actually better than Pac-Man. I spent twenty bucks at the arcade and then went to a restaurant called Jimmy Buffet's Margaritaville. It had gigantic parrots on the outside of it and a real live one inside a golden cage near the bar. Her name was Scarlet and she said, "Make it a double, Pete. BaCAW!" I laughed and told her I thought she was beautiful. I wanted to sit near her but they wouldn't let me sit at the bar because I'm a minor. So I sat at a booth where I could still see Scarlet and ordered a Cheeseburger in Paradise with fries on the side and a chocolate milk. Then my money was gone and it was almost dark, so I said goodbye to Scarlet and went back to the Niagara Motel and checked the phone for a message from Gina. She hadn't called. There was an old message from two days before. A guy named Lester left it for a woman named Chloe. Lester wanted Chloe to meet him in the lobby of the Ramada Inn at ten o'clock and she would know him because he would be wearing jeans and a beige dinner jacket. I erased it and then wished I hadn't. Lester's voice sounded worn-out and fed-up, like he had just watched his whole life go by and realized that he had never really enjoyed any of it. I hoped Chloe had shown up at the Ramada to meet him. I hoped she had been kind to him. I inspected the room for awhile looking for traces of Chloe. Here is what I found:

1. The alarm was set to buzz for seven a.m.

2. Four long black hairs in the bathtub

3. A pink rhinestone earring sparkling behind the toilet

I also found the complimentary pad of paper that said *Niagara Motel* at the top in blue cursive writing, and I did the old detective's trick where you shade a pencil over the page to see what the last person wrote. My heart beat faster as Chloe's writing appeared. 555-7957. The numbers were small and bubbly. There was a double line underneath the phone number and I knew that meant it was important. I wanted to call it and see who would answer. Maybe it would be Lester. Maybe it would be Chloe's friend or her boss. I picked up the phone and let my finger hover above the 5. I ghost-dialed the number to see what shape it would make on the phone. It was a triangle. That was a good sign because the triangle is my favourite shape. It was probably Lester's phone number. I put the receiver back in its cradle. Then I listened to the radio to see which station Chloe had left it on. It was the Classic Rock station. Classic Rock is music that is pretty old, but everyone agrees that it is still good.

While I listened, I unpacked my stuff. I took out my clothes, shook out the wrinkles, folded them again, and put them all into the first two drawers of the brown dresser that the TV sat on. I had two pairs of jeans, a pair of black Adidas trackpants with white stripes up the side, a pair of cut-off jean shorts, five T-shirts, two sweatshirts, and seven pairs of underwear and socks. I didn't have pyjamas because Gina thought pyjamas were a waste of money when you could just wear underwear and a T-shirt to bed. I had two *Choose Your Own Adventure* books: *The Abominable Snowman* and *Trouble on Planet Earth*, the discarded copy of *Where the Red Fern Grows*, and three Archie comics. I had a little shoebox that I kept my beach-glass and special rocks in, my Swiss Army knife that Gina gave me for my tenth birthday, and a brown plastic dog named Charlie. Charlie was the size of my pinky finger and the way his mouth hung open made him look like he was always smiling. I got Charlie out of a gumball machine in Winnipeg, and I'd had him for a long, long time. Except for my birth certificate and my health card, which Gina kept with her stuff, that was everything I had in the world. Gina didn't think we should have too many things since we moved around all the time. She said too much stuff would weigh us down, and I guess she was right. When I finished reading my books, I traded them in at a used bookstore or got more out of a library. When I grew out of my clothes or they got too worn out, Gina bought me more. There were lots of things I wanted, sure, like a skateboard, a Nintendo, a never-ending supply of Bubble Tape, a dog. But Gina said that one day I would have everything I'd ever wanted and then I'd still want more. I'm not really sure what she meant by that, but I think it was her way of telling me that she wasn't going to buy all that stuff for me. Gina had a lot more crap than I did, obviously. She had to have a lot of gear for dancing, a trillion pairs of shoes, a briefcase full of makeup, outfits, wigs, cassette tapes with her special songs on them, a bunch of other junk. I looked at the bags on her bed and thought about unpacking her stuff and putting it away for her, but I turned on the TV instead.

I watched four episodes of *Cheers* back to back. I had seen them all a billion times before but I still laughed along with the live studio audience. *Cheers* is my all-time favourite show. I don't normally tell people this, but there's actually a real possibility that Sam Malone is my father. Gina will never talk about my father so I've pretty much given up asking her about him, but over the years I have been able to find out a few things about him when Gina was half-dreaming or too tired to tell me to leave her alone. These are the reasons I think that Sam Malone might be my real father:

1. My father was a bartender. Sam Malone is a bartender.

2. My father had brown hair. Sam Malone has brown hair.

3. My father was a womanizer. Sam Malone is a womanizer.

4. My father was a recovering alcoholic. Sam Malone is a recovering alcoholic.

5. Our last name is Malone. His last name is Malone.

I know last names don't usually work that way, and I know they weren't married or anything, but still, it's a pretty big coincidence. Also, just because something's on TV doesn't mean it's not real. When I'm old enough to get a job and I can save up enough money, I'm going to take the bus to Boston and go to Sam's bar. I'll walk in and Norm and Woody and Coach will grin their droopy barfly grins at me and Coach will say, "Aren't you a little young to be in here, kid?" And Sam will turn around and he'll be polishing a wine glass with his white bar towel, and when he sees me and realizes who I am, the glass will drop right out of his hand and shatter into a million pieces, but he won't even care, he'll just keep staring at me and his mouth will fall open a little bit. His eyes will start to water, and he'll come out from behind the bar—he'll be trying to talk but he won't be able to say anything because he'll be too emotional—and then he'll kneel down in front of me to look into my eyes and he'll see that they're the very same eyes as his. Then I'll throw my arms around his neck and hug him, real tight, and he'll hug me back. Then we'll slide into a booth and Carla will bring Sam a coffee and me a glass of chocolate milk and she'll be crying too because everyone will be able to see that I'm Sam's son. Norm will drop a little tear in his beer and Coach will get all snuffled up and wipe his eyes with the sleeve of his jacket. Woody will ask, "What's everyone so upset about all of a sudden?" And they'll have to explain it to Woody. They'll have to tell him that I'm Sam's kid and that he's never met me until right now. It might not go exactly like that but it will be some variation of that. They say you never know what's going to happen, but sometimes you have a pretty good idea.

It took a long, long time to fall asleep at the motel because there were fireworks and then the people in the next room kept moaning and banging against the wall, but finally I did fall asleep and when I woke up in the morning the room was cold and Gina still wasn't there.

I opened the curtains and saw an old man in a green rain hat in front of the motel. He stooped down to collect the cigarette butts people had thrown away. He deposited them into a little soup can that was attached to his belt. When he straightened up again, he looked right at me. I didn't know what to do so I gave him a little wave. His face got bright for a moment, and I could almost imagine what he had been like when he was young. Now he looked older than a mummy, and the wrinkles in his face were full of grime. He raised his arm and waved back at me. I could tell by how slowly he did it that he hadn't waved at anyone in a long, long time, almost as if he had forgotten how. A woman wearing pink trackpants was walking a pit bull, and when she passed him, he turned to look at the back of her pants, which said B.U.M. EQUIPMENT across the butt. He kept watching her so I closed the curtains. I got dressed and went out to talk to the front-desk guy to ask if he'd seen Gina. He was flipping through the Yellow Pages. He had a pock-marked face and a tattoo of a scorpion on his neck. He hadn't seen her.

"Did she leave a message for me?"

"Nope."

"Do you guys have a continental breakfast here?"

"Sure don't."

"Oh."

"Anything else?"

"Do you have a waterslide?"

"Nope."

"Well, what kind of amenities *do* you have?"

"Sweet fuck-all," he said.

"Oh. Okay. Thanks."

I was really hungry so I drank a bunch of water and ate two packets of sugar that were in our room with the coffee stuff. Then I walked around for a while to see if Gina was asleep on the sidewalk or a bench, but she wasn't anywhere. It had rained the night before and there were worms all over the road. The air stank of worm. I tried not to step on any of them, but most of them had already been squished. You could hear the robins chirping their little heads off, but you couldn't see them anywhere. They must have been hiding, protecting their babies. A Lincoln Town Car drove by and splashed a huge puddle over me. I got soaked from the knees down. I walked toward the falls. I was tired and wanted to sit down but everything was wet. Then I realized I was already drenched so it didn't really matter anyways. I found a place to sit that was so close to the falls it made my heart stutter. I stared at all that green water rushing over and the silver mist shooting up and wondered what would happen if I jumped in.

People did it.

Some of them died and some of them got famous. Sixteen people have gone over the falls in a barrel or something else. Two of them did it twice. Eleven out of the sixteen survived. That's pretty good odds. But when you look into the river you get dizzy, and you can tell that if you step into it, it will kill you.

I could feel the wetness of the bench seeping through my underwear. My stomach growled and I wished I hadn't spent twenty bucks at the stupid arcade. I wished I knew where Gina was and I wished I knew what to do. It was early and no one was around. As I stared into the white oblivion of the falls, I felt like I was the last human being on earth. I watched the Horseshoe Falls for a long, long time. One million bathtubs of water went over every second. That's probably more baths than I'll have in my whole entire life. In one second. I never knew there was so much water in the world. The sound of it blocked out all the other sounds. The never-ending roar of the falls was so loud that it was overwhelming and I started to get scared that something bad had happened to Gina. She had never not come home before without calling. I stared at the falls that I couldn't turn off and would never ever stop, and I felt like crying or hurling myself at them or both. But then I remembered my horoscope, and I whispered, *I'm in control, I'm in control. I am in control.* Instead of crying or dying, I went back to the motel and asked scorpion guy to borrow the phonebook. Then I went to our room and called the Greater Niagara General Hospital.

# 3

A lady doctor named Dr Chopra came to get me in the waiting room. She had dark hair stuck up in a tight bun and gave me a little smile with no teeth. We took the elevator to the third floor, and she led me through the fluorescent hallways to a blue room where I saw Gina lying in a bed. She had two black eyes and her nose was all swollen, her head was wrapped in a white bandage, and she had tubes and wires going in and out of her arms and a tube coming out of her chest. I started to cry.

"Is this your mother?" Dr Chopra asked.

I nodded.

"Can you tell me her name?"

"Gina. Gina Malone."

She nodded. "Good." She put her hand on my shoulder. "Tucker, your mom was hit by a mini-van last night. The driver said she was lying in the road and he didn't see her until it was too late."

I moved away so her hand wasn't on my shoulder anymore.

"She's in serious but stable condition. Her right leg was crushed, and she has a fractured pelvis. She has three broken ribs and a collapsed lung. Her nose is broken too."

"But, she's ... is she ... ?"

"She's going to live, yes. But it will take a long time for her to make a full recovery."

"How long?"

"Well, because she has bruising on her heart, I'll need to keep her here for at least a couple of weeks. Maybe three, depending on how her lung is healing." Dr Chopra opened the closet and took Gina's purse off a hook. "This was found with her, in case you need anything out of it."

"Okay." I hugged the purse against my chest.

"Do you have any family you can call? Anyone you can stay with?"

"Gina's my family."

Dr Chopra nodded.

"She has narcolepsy," I said.

"I see," Dr Chopra said.

"That's probably why she was in the road. She probably had a sleep attack. She's supposed to take her roofies but she forgets to get the prescription filled and runs out all the time. I keep telling her she needs to always take them but ... " I wiped my nose on my sleeve.

Dr Chopra wrote something on Gina's chart then turned back to me. "Well, you're welcome to stay here tonight and I'll make sure someone from Child and Family Services comes and sees you first thing tomorrow. Oh, and I'll give you these meal tickets for the cafeteria downstairs." She handed me a roll of coupons.

"Thanks."

"There are blankets in the closet here and just let the nurses know if you need anything."

"Okay."

"Right. Well, I'll be back later on to check on her. Push that buzzer if she wakes up, okay?"

"Okay."

Dr Chopra left, and I stood in the corner and stared at Gina. She looked small and pale. I thought of the albino pigeon that used to nest on our motel balcony in Nanaimo. I went over to stand next to Gina's bed and watched the mint-green sheet rise and fall with her breathing machine. The breathing machine was loud and sounded like whooshing water. I got dizzy after a while and had to sit down. My stomach hurt so I went to the cafeteria to eat.

When I came back, I got some blankets out of the closet and set up the chairs so I could stretch out on them and rest my head on the edge of the bed. I fell asleep thinking about the guy in the mini-van who ran over Gina. I wondered where he was now and what he was doing. I wondered if he had ever heard of narcolepsy. I wondered if he had a mom.

\*\*\*

In the middle of the night, I woke up to Gina's fingers running through my hair. I sat up.

"Hi," she whispered.

"Hi."

She smiled at me and my heart burst. She was alive. She was alive and she could talk and she knew who I was and she was broken but she would be okay. I told her everything Dr Chopra had told me; that she was fractured and crushed and collapsed. I told her that her heart was bruised. She put her hand on her chest and looked down to where her heart was, as if she'd be able to see it through her body.

"Should I push the button now to tell them you woke up?"

"No."

"Are you scared?"

"No."

"How come?"

"Because you're here now." She reached for my hand then, and we stayed like that, holding hands, until we both fell asleep.

# 4

It was decided that I would stay at a group home for kids called Bright Light while Gina was recovering. Really, the house was meant for teenagers, but Collette, the social worker, said it would be okay because I would only be staying there temporarily while Gina recovered. Collette had short brown hair that curled up against her forehead like fiddlehead ferns. We sat across from each other in the hospital cafeteria. Collette drank peppermint tea out of a paper cup. I drank chocolate milk out of a carton.

"I'm only eleven, you know."

"I know that, Tucker. But I think you're very mature for your age."

"Really?"

"Yes, I do."

"I still make fart noises with my armpit."

"Well," she smiled. "You know when it's not appropriate to do that too."

"I still watch cartoons."

"That's fine."

"Are you sure I can live with fifteen-to-eighteen-year-olds?"

"It's only for a few weeks, and unfortunately there are no spots available in foster care right now, so this is really the best option for you. I'm sure you'll get along just fine at Bright Light."

"But I want to stay here, with Gina."

"I'm sorry, Tucker, but you can't do that."

"Then let me stay at the motel. Chad can keep an eye on me."

"Who's Chad?"

"Chad's the front-desk guy at the Niagara Motel. He has a scorpion tattoo on his neck."

Collette pressed her lips together.

When I'd called the hospital and found out that Gina was there, Chad had taped a sign on the front door of the motel that said **BACK IN 15 MINITS!** I didn't think it was important that he had spelled minutes wrong, so I didn't mention it. Chad drove me to the hospital in his black Chevrolet Caprice. He lit a cigarette and rolled his window down an inch. I said thanks for the ride and he said no problem. He had told me he was trying to be a good person now, and that driving a kid to the hospital to see his mom who had just been in an accident was something a good person would do.

Despite all this, Collette would not agree to me staying on at the motel. She also told me that she had registered me for school and that I would start at Niagara Elementary on Monday.

"Do you even know what grade I'm in?"

"Grade six," she said.

"Okay."

I didn't completely hate school, but I didn't love it either. School is just one of those things you have to do until you get old enough not to.

I went back upstairs to say goodbye to Gina. She was sleeping and I wanted to wake her up so she would know what was going on, but I also knew that she should rest because resting helps you heal. I left her a note explaining about Bright Light and put it on the bedside table. In the note, I promised that I would be back tomorrow to visit her. I drew a heart on it, but then I thought that might make her think of her own heart being bruised and that would make her sad. So I erased it and drew a little cartoon of a farmer riding a donkey with a broken foreleg and the farmer saying, *I broke my ass*, because laughter is the best medicine. I watched Gina for a minute, all pale and broken like a crushed moth. A machine breathing for her. A machine feeding her. I hated to see her like that. It made my insides feel like they could drop right out my butt at any moment. I gave her a kiss on the forehead and told her I loved her, which I never usually said, but since she was asleep it didn't really matter anyways.

# 5

Collette was totally wrong about me fitting in at Bright Light. I looked *so* much younger than all the other kids that nobody talked to me, nobody even wanted to be *seen* talking to me, except to say things like, "Watch it, ass-maggot," after they trampled over me in the hallway, or, "Are you even potty-trained yet?" if they saw me in line for the bathroom. It wasn't my fault I was born five or six or seven years after they were, I just wasn't conceived yet. No one gets to choose when they're born. The fact that none of the kids spoke to me based on my birth date was completely unfair. But no one considers justice in a place like that.

On my second day there I stood in front of the fridge, looking inside it. I'm not sure what for. A blond, pimply guy named Josh came up behind me and shut the fridge.

"Are your parents married?" Josh asked me.

"No," I said.

"Ha, you're a bastard." He laughed and punched me in the arm, hard.

"So?"

"You gonna cry? Little bastard gonna cry?"

"No."

He slapped me across the face. "Can you fight?"

"No."

He slapped me again. "Can you run?"

"No."

He slapped me again. "Well, what *can* you do?"

"Nothing," I said, my eyes hot with tears.

"I knew it! You're a little bastard who can't do nothing!"

I ran out of the kitchen before he could hit me again.

I knew I was a bastard a long time ago because this smart girl named Claire Christakos in Winnipeg had told me about it in grade two. But it didn't matter. Lots of people were bastards. There are actually two different kinds of bastards, and the other kind has nothing to do with your parents.

Because it was a warm spring, I spent most of my time outside, cruising the strip and watching people, watching the falls, and watching people watch the falls. I probably saw people take a bajillion pictures of the falls, and I was even in a few of them too. But it was good that people were taking pictures, because every day Niagara Falls looked a little bit different, and who would remember exactly what they had looked like the day before or the week before or the month before if there were no pictures out there for photo evidence?

I visited Gina in the hospital every day after school from three to five p.m., which were the visiting hours. On Saturdays and Sundays I could stay from one to five p.m., and then Gina and I would watch a movie or play Boggle or I would read to her or give her a *Cosmo* quiz, and then I wouldn't feel so lonely. Gina had a roommate named Mrs Jorgenson who was old and shriveled and coughed up phlegm all the time and spit it into a glass jar that she kept beside her bed. Mrs Jorgenson didn't speak very much English. She sometimes hollered at Gina to turn the TV off or turn the volume down or change the channel, and she always yelled for the nurse instead of pushing the white button on the wall above the bed like you were supposed to. Gina said that even though Mrs Jorgenson was crabby and yelled at us, we should always be extra nice to her because she might not be leaving the hospital. I was lying next to Gina on her bed and we were watching *The Golden Girls*, which we thought was Mrs Jorgenson's favourite show because she always hacked up a lung and a half while laughing when we watched it.

"You mean she has to stay here for the rest of her life?" I whispered.

"I mean, she might not have many days left in her life," Gina whispered.

"Oh."

Gina nodded and smoothed my hair. She gave me a little kiss on the head, and I curled in to her as close as I could without touching her ribs.

Gina had given me all the money in her purse, $226.38, so that I could buy lunch and go to the arcade, and get some of those shiny bouncy balls with the little creatures inside them that she knew I liked.

"Maybe if you bought something you could share with your house-mates, that would help break the ice," she suggested.

"Like what?"

"I don't know, candy?"

"*Candy?*"

"What?"

"Gina, they're *teenagers!* They don't like *candy!*"

"Everyone likes candy."

"You don't get it."

"Look, I'm sorry it's so sucky in there. I wish it didn't have to be this way. I'd change it if I could, Tucker."

"I know."

"You're just going to have to make the best of it. It's not going to be forever. Just a couple more weeks."

"A couple *more* weeks?"

She nodded. "Dr Chopra says she needs to keep an eye on me for a little bit longer."

"Well, just tell her that you're ready to go."

"I did. She said that's fine but my heart's not ready yet."

"That's dumb."

She turned to look at me. "Did they tell you that I died?"

"No."

"Well, I did."

"What the frig are you talking about? You're right here, you jerk." I poked her in the arm.

"I went into cardiac arrest and was clinically dead for almost two minutes."

"No way."

"Way. They had to restart my heart with the heart-charger thingy."

"Why didn't you tell me?"

"I thought you knew."

"Well, I didn't."

"Do you know what they call it when your heart stops like that?"

"What?"

"A Code Blue."

"Code Blue?"

"Yep."

"Blue's my favourite colour," I said.

"I know."

"So ... what was it like?"

"Being dead?"

"Yeah, I mean ... did you see anything?"

"You mean like God sitting on a cloud or angels playing harps?"

"I don't know! You're the one who died!"

"No. I didn't see anything. But I felt something."

"What?"

"I felt ... nothing."

"*What?*"

"Emptiness."

"Emptiness?"

"Yep. Just this clear and total emptiness. Like, there was no me, there was no world, there was no nothing, just blank."

"No me?"

"Not even you."

I thought about that for a minute. "Kind of like a chalkboard after it's been erased?"

"Like no chalkboard being there at all."

"Huh."

"Yeah."

We stared up at the ceiling. I wondered what it would be like to feel empty. It sounded kind of nice. I closed my eyes and tried to clear my head, but stupid thoughts kept bonking around, and I could feel that my body was there, and I could feel that Gina was there breathing beside me, her arm against my arm, and I liked her being there, and if I were empty, I wouldn't be able to do this, to feel this, because I would be nothing. Then I remembered that Gina had died. And I didn't ever want that to happen ever, ever again. A tear slipped out of the corner of my eye, but I brushed it away before she could see.

"Gina?"

"Yeah?"

"You can't die again."

"Okay." She curled a piece of my hair around her finger.

"Promise."

"Not for a long, long time."

"Not ever."

"Well, I can't promise that."

# 6

The other kids at Bright Light weren't there because their parent was in the hospital. They were there because their parent was in jail or dead or an alcoholic or a drug addict or beat the living snot out of them. They were there because no one loved them enough to let them live with them. And even if someone *did* love them enough, that someone didn't trust them. I knew all this because I had what one of my grade-four teachers, Ms Wesley, called Amazing Powers of Observation. Which is not the same as having X-Ray Vision or Being Able to Predict the Future, but at least it was something. Also, I was good at blending into my surroundings, so I could listen to the kids talk and watch them interact with each other without them really noticing that I was there.

I knew that the leader of the kids was Leo. Leo was eighteen and had a buzz cut. He had a big red goatee that made him look way older than eighteen, and he had black letters tattooed on the knuckles of both of his hands. His right hand said HARD and his left hand said CORE, and I guess that's what Leo was. He'd been to juvie three times for selling drugs and stealing cars. Now that he was eighteen, he could be tried in court as an adult so he was trying to stay out of trouble. You could tell he wasn't trying *that* hard, though. Leo's mom lived in a crack-house in Niagara Falls and his dad lived in St. Catherines with his second wife and their two kids. Leo hated the two kids, the second wife, and his dad. I'm not sure why. Anyone who's lucky enough to have a dad should at least try not to hate him. One of the reasons I knew that Leo was the most powerful of all the kids in the house was because whenever he would walk into a room, everyone would shut up. And it wasn't because they were talking about him. It was because they knew that whatever they were saying wasn't important enough for Leo to have to hear. Another reason I could tell that Leo was the leader was because kids were always trying to suck up to him. Like they would automatically give him cigarettes whenever he asked instead of saying they only had one left or they didn't have any, which is what they said to everyone else who asked. And when we ate together in the dining room around the big oak table, everyone would wait for Leo to start eating before digging in. Even the staff members sucked up to Leo, and no one ever gave him trouble for wearing his combat boots in the house or not getting in before curfew or not doing his chore on the chore wheel. Sometimes the other kids would do Leo's chore *for* him so he wouldn't have to do it, that's how big of a deal this guy was.

The kid who I figured was the lowest on the totem pole before I got there was a guy named Daryl. Everyone called him Dirtbag Daryl. Daryl was fifteen but looked younger. He smelled like wet socks and never combed his hair. He had so many freckles it looked like someone had splashed a bucket of mud all over him. He talked a lot and kicked chair legs and table legs and knocked over cups of water. He said rude things to everyone, especially the girls. He was constantly looking for something he'd lost—his key, his lighter, his pack of beef jerky—and he'd shoot into a room like a Roman candle.

I could tell from the way he laughed, with his head tipped back and his mouth wide open, that Daryl wasn't actually a mean person, it was just all he had going for him. Being mean, loud, and annoying, that was his shtick. Gina says everyone has to have a shtick. If Daryl didn't have that, he'd be nothing. Just a foot-tapping, finger-drumming, red-headed mess of freckles that nobody cared about. Even if they were only telling him to shut the hell up, at least people talked to him. Once, I asked Dirtbag Daryl why his knees always bounced around like crazy when he was sitting in a chair, and he said, "You'll find out when you're older." People usually say stuff like that when it has something to do with sex, but I know you don't use your knees to do sex so I'm not really sure what he meant. I guess I'll have to wait and see.

Basically, I just tried to keep out of everybody's way. I read some of the books that were on the bookshelf: *Catch-22*, *To Kill a Mockingbird*, and *The Authoritative Calvin and Hobbes*. I watched TV when everyone else did but I never got to pick the channel. Sometimes someone would switch it to *Cheers*, and I would be glad for it.

There was a girl who lived at Bright Light with long black hair who looked familiar, but I couldn't figure out why. Her name was Meredith, and she was sixteen. She wore dark makeup around her eyes and baggy black hoodies and didn't say too much to anyone. She had a nose ring, which was kind of gross, but kind of cool too. I knew she liked *Cheers* because she would laugh when it was on. I knew that she liked to read because I saw her staring at the bookshelf one day. She looked as if choosing her next book was the most important decision she would ever make. I wanted to wait and see which one she would pick, but it got awkward just standing behind her in the hallway while she stared at all the books so I went and watched Kyle and Shawn play foosball for a while. I asked if I could play, and they pretended not to hear me. I asked again, louder, and Kyle scored a point on Shawn. Then Shawn picked up the ball and looked at me and said, "If you *ever* talk to me again I'm going to shove this ball so far up your ass it's going to pop out your eyeball." Kyle laughed and said, "Beat it, anus-face," and they kept playing. I went to my room and got into bed. I stared at the underside of the top bunk where someone had written FUCK THE WORLD 'CUZ THE WORLD IS FUCKED!!! in black Magic Marker. I closed my eyes. I wished that I didn't have to be in here with all these mean-ass teenagers, and I wished that Gina wasn't in the hospital so she could take me to Marineland. I thought about dolphins doing flips. I thought about seals barking.

Then I thought about dogs barking. Then I remembered something Norm said on a recent episode of *Cheers*: "It's a dog-eat-dog world, Sammy, and I'm wearing Milk-Bone underwear."

Then I started feeling a little bit better, because everyone has to wear Milk-Bone underwear sometimes. I thought about Sam for awhile and wondered what kind of dog he would have. Probably a border collie since they're the smartest. And even though people like Diane are always giving Sam a hard time about being stupid, he's not actually stupid, not when it comes to people. He's actually really smart. Plus, he stopped drinking and turned his life around. Stupid people wouldn't be able to do that. Stupid people can't see their way out of their own problems. But maybe Sam would have a mutt, because that would suit him too.

I knew that Sam didn't know that Gina was pregnant with me or else he never would have left. But one day soon I would find him, and he'd feel so sad and sorry for leaving and missing out on my whole life that maybe he would even get me a dog of my own. Sam would let me work at the bar sometimes. I'd help him polish glasses and change the kegs, and he'd let me bring the dog to work. The dog would sleep behind the bar or else rest his head in Coach's lap. Rebecca wouldn't like my dog at first—she'd complain about him all the time and she and Sam would fight about it—but eventually, she'd grow to love him. I'd teach him to sit and roll over and jump up and give me a hug and he'd be the best dog in the whole entire world.

I thought about my dog for a good while and what I would name him, but I couldn't decide without meeting him first. After a while I got out of my bunk and went downstairs.

Meredith was sitting on the stairs drinking a can of Coke and reading *Watership Down*. I knew which book she had finally chosen, and I knew I would read it next. Because even if you don't really know a person, you can sort of figure them out a bit by reading the same books they've read. I'm not exactly sure what makes girls pretty or women beautiful, but I could see that Meredith had it, whatever *it* was. Her eyes were green as grass and her face was a nice shape, not square or pug-like, just round and smooth and nice to look at. She wasn't fat, but she wasn't like the girl in the Calvin Klein commercials, either. She was solid, like a tree trunk. I went back upstairs, not because I had to, but because I wanted to pass by her again. She didn't glance up or move over or anything and I wondered if I had been blending into my surroundings so well for so long that I had actually become invisible.

*** 

My grade-six teacher at Niagara Elementary was Mr Zabriskie. He was old and had grey tufts of hair poking out the sides of his head like a koala bear. He wore brown cardigans and drank out of a coffee mug that smelled like Listerine. He was so boring that he even bored himself, and he yawned all the time. I think he was going deaf, too. Either that or he pretended not to hear us. Nobody in my class really talked to me, and I didn't make too much of an effort to talk to anyone either. At recess I did pull-ups on the monkey bars or read my book or drew comics, and at lunchtime I went downtown and walked around. The truth was that no one in my class was even half as interesting as the kids in the group home.

One day, I was walking around downtown during lunch-hour, and I saw Meredith. She was leaning up against a brick wall in front of a cigar shop twirling her hair around her finger. She wore a short jean skirt with black pantyhose underneath. Her pantyhose had big holes all over them. Then I remembered where I had seen Meredith before. Standing on that same corner. Wearing a tight dress. Leaning into car windows. She looked bored, so I went up to her to say hi and see if she wanted to get a Slurpee or something.

"Get lost, kid," she said.

"Your name's Meredith, right?"

"Get out of here. I mean it."

"I just wanted to say hi."

"Hi."

"Hi."

"*Hi*, okay? Now scram. I'm trying to work here."

"Oh."

A brown station wagon pulled up to the curb and a guy wearing a Blue Jays hat rolled down the window. Meredith stood up, away from the wall. "*Fuck off*," she said to me out of the side of her mouth.

I spun on my heel and fast-walked away. When I looked back, I saw Meredith sliding into the passenger seat of the station wagon.

I walked around the block twice but didn't see the brown station wagon anywhere. I knew what Meredith was doing. Pretty sure. I went to the 7-Eleven and got two Coke Slurpees then walked back to the cigar shop. Meredith was back. She was leaning against the wall smoking a cigarette.

"I got this for you." I held out the Slurpee to her.

"Really?"

"Yeah. I thought maybe you could use a refreshment."

"Thanks, kid. That's sweet." Her nose ring glinted in the sunlight. She took the Slurpee from me.

"My name's Tucker." I stuck out my hand.

"Meredith."

We shook hands.

"Are you hungry, Meredith?"

"Starving."

"I was on my way to get something for lunch. There's this hot dog stand down by the falls—"

"Sure." She took another sip of her Slurpee and then started down the hill. Her legs were longer than mine, and she walked fast and I had to hurry to keep up. We passed a bunch of wide-eyed tourists, we passed a screaming baby whose mom looked like her head was about to explode, we passed a group of skater kids and one of them spit so close to Meredith his phlegm-wad nearly hit her leg. She gave him the finger but didn't slow down.

We both put sauerkraut and mustard and ketchup and relish on our hot dogs. Meredith also put banana peppers on hers. Banana peppers make my stomach hurt so I don't eat them anymore. And besides, they don't even taste like bananas. We sat on a bench near the statue of Nikola Tesla and looked out over the falls as we ate. The sun was sharp in my eyes and I thought about buying Terminator sunglasses I had seen earlier in the 7-Eleven. Meredith finished her hot dog, wiped her chin with her napkin, and let out a gigantic burp. She didn't say excuse me.

"How old are you anyways?" she squinted at me.

"Eleven."

"Jesus."

"Tucker."

She laughed. "Why are you at Lite Brite?"

"My mom."

"Crack fiend?"

"No."

"Alcoholic?"

"Uh-uh."

"Klepto!"

"What's that?"

"When you have an irresistible compulsion to steal things."

"No. She doesn't have that. She has narcolepsy."

Meredith snickered. "She has sex with dead people?"

"No! *Ew!*"

Meredith laughed.

"She has a condition. It makes her fall asleep when she shouldn't. She falls asleep a lot. And she also gets these attacks where she's not really asleep. She just can't move or talk or anything. It's called cataplexy. She can't control it."

"And they took you away for that?"

"No. Not for that. They took me away because she passed out in the middle of the road and got run over by a mini-van and now she's in the hospital."

"No shit."

"It's very serious. She has bruising on her heart."

"That sucks."

"She actually died for two minutes. But they brought her back."

"No way."

"Code Blue, it's called."

"*Shit.*"

We stared out at the thundering water. A seagull sailed over us and dropped a crap on Nikola Tesla's head.

"What did your mom say about it?"

"About dying?"

"Yeah."

"She said it was like there's no chalkboard at all."

"What is she, a teacher or something?"

"No."

"What's her job?"

"She's sort of like you, I guess."

Meredith looked at me for a too-long second. Then she picked at a hole in her pantyhose.

"Mostly she dances at clubs and stuff, but she also does ... the other things. Sometimes."

"So, you know what I do?"

"I guess." I shrugged.

"And your mom does it too?"

"Sometimes. Mostly just dancing."

"You mean stripping."

"Exotic dancing."

"Stripping. She's a stripper."

I shrugged.

Meredith took out a cigarette. She watched me out of the corner of her eye while she lit it. "You want one?"

I looked out to the falls, at all the white mist billowing up. It was like a giant cloud was trapped inside the waterfall and wanted nothing more than to get back up to the sky with its other cloud friends. "Sure." I took the cigarette from her and stuck it between my lips. She flicked her lighter, and I leaned toward the flame. Her lighter was black and so were her fingernails. I blew out a mini-cloud of smoke and coughed. I had smoked before, once, in Prince George, behind the grade-six portable, after school with Bryce. It was a menthol cigarette he had stolen from his mom. I smoked half of it, then puked in a garbage can while Bryce laughed at me and smoked the rest. This time wasn't so bad though, because Meredith didn't smoke menthols. She smoked Export A Gold. And also because I wasn't really inhaling, I was just trying to make little smoke clouds. Meredith blew a smoke ring like it was the easiest thing in the world.

"Take a picture, it lasts longer," she said.

"Sorry."

She blew another white o that floated above my head. "Where are you from, kid?"

"I don't know."

"Come on, you don't know where you're from?"

"Paris, I guess." I tapped my cigarette and the ash drifted down and dissolved into the grass.

"*Paris?* You speak French, then?"

"Paris, Ontario."

"*Ah.* But of *course*," she said in a French accent.

"But I've lived a lot of different places. I've gone to sixteen different schools. That's why I said I don't know."

"Where have you lived the longest?"

"I'm not sure. I'd have to ask Gina."

"Gina's your mom?"

"Yep."

"What's her stripper name?"

"Angel."

"Angel," Meredith smiled. "That's a good one."

"Do you use another name?"

She took a drag that lasted an age, then said, "Mary."

"That's a nice name."

"You like it?"

"Yeah."

"I don't really like it. I thought that it might make the johns be nicer to me. Even if it's only subconsciously."

"You mean because Jesus's mom's name was Mary?"

"Yep."

We laughed. A kid rode by us on a shiny silver unicycle and Meredith whistled at him. I wished that I had a unicycle. If I had a unicycle, all of my problems would be solved.

"I like Angel, though. It's pretty. People would be nice to an Angel."

"Yeah, they probably would," I said.

"Are people nice to your mom?"

"I think so," I said.

"So," Meredith said. "You're from nowhere and everywhere, eh?"

"I guess."

"Where was the last place you lived?"

"Prince George."

"Never heard of it." She blew smoke out the side of her mouth.

"It's in northern British Columbia."

"BC's cool."

"Yeah. Prince George isn't, though."

"Where else have you lived?"

"Um, Winnipeg, Regina, Medicine Hat, Calgary, Red Deer, Moose Jaw, Edmonton, Vancouver, Nanaimo, Thunder Bay, Sudbury... some other places. What about you?"

"I'm from Toronto."

"Cool."

Meredith took a hard drag off her cigarette.

"How come you came here?"

"Too many people there. I didn't like feeling crowded all the time."

"I don't like crowds either," I said.

"Plus, the waterfalls are supposed to be good for you."

"Good how?"

"Apparently, if you're around a lot of water, it gives off these negative ions, and it makes you feel better, it makes you feel happy."

"Oh. So ... are you?"

"What, happy?"

"Yeah."

She took a puff, exhaled. "I don't know. Is anyone?"

I shrugged. "I don't know. I guess, sometimes, maybe."

Meredith tapped her cigarette. The wind ruffled the ends of her hair against her shoulders. She didn't look sad to me, she looked ... thoughtful. She looked like maybe she'd had more of life than other kids her age, but she was wiser for it.

"Do you like being sixteen?" I asked.

Meredith exhaled a thin stream of smoke out toward the falls. She nodded slowly, her eyes glazed over as she stared into the green crush of water. "It's okay." She stood up and let her cigarette fall to the ground. "I have to get back to work," she said. The cigarette rolled away and smoked itself from a crack in the sidewalk.

"Okay." I stood up.

I felt dizzy, as if the mist-cloud trapped in the falls had landed on my head and gone inside my brain. Meredith began to walk. I dropped my cigarette on the sidewalk and wondered if the old man in the green rain hat would find it and put it into his soup can. I hurried to catch up with Meredith until she stopped to tie her shoelace. She had the same shoes as me, black and white Converse sneakers. But hers were high-tops and came up past her ankle. When we got close to the cigar shop she said, "See ya later, kid." I knew that was my cue to leave although I didn't want to. What I wanted to do was sit on that bench in front of the statue of Nikola Tesla and talk with Meredith all day. I wanted to ask her if she had ever felt happy. I wanted to ask her if her hair was really that black or if she got it out of a box of Nice 'n Easy. I wanted to ask her if she had poked all the holes in her pantyhose on purpose or if they just got that way over time. I wanted to ask her why she was at Bright Light and what *her* mom's job was. I wanted to ask her to be my friend. But instead I said, "Okay," shoved my hands in my pockets, and kept walking.

1

After school, I went to see Gina. She was lying on her back staring up at the ceiling, her sky-blue eyes all glassy and blank. For a second, I thought she was dead. A sinkhole in the floor opened up beneath me and started to swallow everything that ever was. The chairs and all the machines and the IV stand got sucked down into the hungry hole. Then Gina's pinky finger moved, and I could breathe again and the floor closed up and everything went back to its place. She was sleeping with her eyes open, which she sometimes did, but I had forgotten. I wondered if she was sleeping like a normal person or if she'd had a sleep attack. I went to the vending machine and bought a pack of Skittles. Then I went to the nurse's station and talked to Heather, the fat nurse with the black hairs growing out of her chin. Heather wore scrubs with hearts and teddy bears on them and she usually gave me a honey-dip donut on Saturdays if there were any left. She was the nicest nurse in there. I had thought that all nurses would be nice, but it's not true. Most of them are too busy to even say hi, and some of them scowled at me if I came in after visiting hours. Heather said Gina had been like that for awhile and they knew she was narcoleptic so they just made sure that she was breathing and her heart was beating, and they let her sleep with her eyes open.

"Do you want to wake her up?" Heather asked.

I shrugged and offered Heather some Skittles.

"No thanks, hon. I'm trying a new diet."

"The kind where you eat less and exercise more?"

She laughed. "Something like that."

"Because that's the only kind of diet that works."

She smiled for a millisecond then held out her hand, and I poured a pile of Skittles into it.

"When is Dr Chopra going to let Gina out of here?"

"I don't know, sweetie."

"Can I talk to her?"

"To Dr Chopra?"

"Yeah."

Heather looked down at her clipboard, then back up at me. "She's not in today."

"What do you mean?"

"It's her day off."

"But she's a doctor."

"Everyone gets a day off once in awhile, kiddo."

"Not me."

"Do you have a job?"

"Yeah, the hardest job there is."

"What's that?"

"Being a kid."

"Ha! You think that's hard, you should try being a woman!" She popped the whole handful of Skittles into her mouth and smiled big at me to show me her rainbow teeth as she chewed them up. I laughed and showed her a mouth-rainbow too.

***

That night the dinner at Bright Light was pork chops, boiled potatoes, and broccoli. But the pork chops were overdone and rubber-chewy and Dirtbag Daryl kept going on about how everyone was masticating so hard and how the pork chops were really difficult to masticate. He kept saying masticate this and masticate that, and at first it was really obnoxious and people told him to shut the hell up. Meredith threw a piece of broccoli at him but he kept on doing it and eventually everyone started cracking up, even Brian, who was the SOD, which stands for Staff On Duty. The word masticate means chew and it sounds like the word masturbate which means jerking-off for boys and humping a pillow for girls. I pictured a girl humping a pork chop which is totally ridiculous, so then I started cracking up too. I looked around the table at everyone laughing. Kyle's face was turning red, Jayleen was choking on her milk from laughing so hard, and Josh was snorting like a pig, which made everyone laugh even harder, and for a minute, you could almost believe that we were a regular family, just sitting around the table, masticating our pork chops, laughing at our idiot brother. The laugh session seemed to go on and on, and I was glad Gina wasn't there because she always gets a sleep attack when she laughs hard like that. Finally, it faded out. Shawn moaned. Tiffany wiped tears from her eyes. Then everyone got really quiet, even Dirtbag Daryl. There was a strange heaviness upon us, like someone had just made us all a promise that we knew they couldn't keep. Kids started to get up and put their plates in the dishwasher. Chairs scraped against the tile floor as people shoved themselves away from the table. I sat at the table staring down at my plate until everyone had left the dining room. I pushed my broccoli stumps around in a circle and waited for the heavy feeling to go away. After awhile, Brian, the SOD, came back in. He tucked in all the chairs but one and then sat in it, across the table from me.

"How are you doing, kid?"

"Okay."

"Yeah?"

I shrugged.

"How's your mom?"

"Not good. Her heart's bruised. Bad."

"She's going to get better though, right?"

"She could die if things don't heal properly." Saying it made my legs feel watery, but I knew it was true. I made a pillow with my elbows and put my head down. I kept looking at Brian with one eye.

Brian scratched his beard. It was brown and thick and made him look like a wannabe lumberjack. Or maybe he was a lumberjack when he wasn't supervising juveniles. It's hard to tell what people do in their spare time just by looking at them. But I was pretty sure that Brian wasn't a lumberjack. He wore a Nirvana T-shirt. The one with a yellow smiley face on it and x's for eyes. "I know it must be hard in here for you sometimes," he said.

"Most of the time."

"But you know what?"

"What?"

"You're one of the lucky ones."

"Oh yeah?"

"Yeah, man. You're going to be leaving soon, to live with your mom."

"So?"

"So some of these kids don't ever get to leave."

"You mean they have to stay here for their whole life?"

"Well, until they're nineteen, then they have to move out and look after themselves for the rest of their life."

"Get jobs?"

"Yep, get jobs, find a place to live, buy groceries, make food, pay bills, all that."

"Can kids have jobs?"

"That depends."

"On what?" I thought of Meredith, working her corner. She probably made more money than some adults did.

"Well, it depends on what you want to do. See, kids under fourteen aren't supposed to work for a company or a store or a restaurant, but it's okay for kids your age to do other work, like mow lawns, babysit, deliver newspapers, stuff like that."

"Brian?"

"Yeah?"

"Do you think that *I* could get a job?"

"I don't see why not."

"But not some crap job. I need to make a lot of money."

"Why's that?"

"Because I need to go find my father."

"Why's that?"

"Because he's my *father*."

Brian squinted at me, waiting.

"And because, if something happens to Gina, I mean, if she doesn't get better, or if she has another accident, then ... "

"Okay." Brian nodded. He swallowed and his Adam's apple bounced in his throat like a super-bouncy ball. "Do you know where he lives?"

"I think maybe Boston. I think he might own a bar there."

"Shouldn't be too hard to track him down then," Brian said.

# 8

I made up signs to cut people's lawns and posted them all over town, but nobody ever called. Or else maybe someone *did* call, but no one at the group home gave me the message. I phoned the *Niagara Gazette* about doing a paper route, but they told me they already had enough carriers in my area. I thought about collecting bottles and cans and cashing them in, but then I remembered that guys here do that for a living and that's how they buy their food and pay for their clothes and stuff and if I collected bottles, wouldn't that kind of be like stealing from them? Plus, it took all day to make a few bucks, anyways. I kind of gave up looking for a job, but I didn't give up on the idea of one day going to Boston to find Sam Malone.

Sometimes, when I was hanging around downtown, I'd lean up against a building and watch people walk by. I used to imagine that I'd see Sam coming toward me and I'd wait for him to recognize me, his own flesh and blood. But then, it wouldn't be him, it would just be some regular schmo, and then I'd wait for the next man who looked like my father to walk toward me.

I bugged Gina about it for the zillionth time. We lay on her bed watching *Wheel of Fortune*. One of the contestants was a tall man with light brown hair.

"Is that what my father looks like?"

"Who?"

"That guy in the middle. Gary."

"No."

"What does he look like?"

"I don't know. I haven't seen him since before you were born."

"Well, what *did* he look like then?"

"Tucker," she rubbed my head. "I'm trying to watch, okay?"

Gary spun the wheel and it landed on BANKRUPT. The crowd *ooohed* as he pouted.

"I just want to know what he looked like! You could at least tell me *that*. Do I even look like him?"

"No," she said. "You're fair. He was dark."

"What else?"

"Tucker, he's out of the picture, all right? Just don't worry about him."

"How can I not worry about him?"

"You don't really need a father, you know," she whispered. Vanna turned a letter, grinning like a maniac.

"All the other kids have one."

"If all the other kids had scurvy would you want that, too?"

"I don't know. What is it?"

"Scurvy?"

"Yeah."

"Scurvy is when you don't eat enough fruits and vegetables and your skin turns yellow and your teeth fall out and eventually you die."

"That can happen?"

"Sure."

"Yeah, right. You're just telling me that so I'll eat my vegetables. And besides, it's different. It's not the same thing. It's apples and oranges."

Gina laughed. "It's the truth," she said. "Cross my heart and hope to die."

"I have to get going." I climbed off the bed and started to look for my shoes.

"Aw, really? You just got here. Can't you stay a little longer?"

"No, I have homework."

"Oh, okay," she said. She smiled. "I'm glad you're doing your homework."

I shrugged.

"What's it in?"

"Math," I said. "Long division."

She nodded.

"It's pretty easy."

"Okay. Good. Well, you go do it then."

I put on my shoes. "See ya later, Gina."

***

I started going to Meredith's corner every day at lunchtime to see if she wanted to eat with me. Sometimes she wasn't there, so I'd sit and wait or walk around the block a few times until she came back. She always came back. She never told me to get lost again, but we always left her spot in front of the cigar shop straight away. This was how Meredith and I started having lunch together every day. We were a strange match as far as friends go, but magnets don't need to understand how magnetism works; they just repel each other or stick together.

Meredith didn't talk to me too much when we were at the group home, but she wasn't mean to me either. When she was there, she mostly just read and watched TV and so did I. For lunch we'd go to Burger King or KFC or McDonald's or the hot dog stand. Sometimes she'd buy lunch for both of us and sometimes she wouldn't. It depended on what kind of morning she'd had and how flush she was. Once, I offered to buy her lunch and she said, "Your money's no good here, sir," and slid the five bucks back in my pocket.

Meredith told me that she was trying to raise money to pay her brother's bail. Her brother's name was Steve and he was twenty-one. Steve was in the Don Jail in Toronto for selling cocaine. His bail was set at $100,000, and none of his scumbag friends would pay it for him so Meredith had to come up with a way to raise the money on her own. She didn't tell me how much she had already saved and I didn't ask. People get weird when you talk about money, as if how much money they have is equal to how much they're worth inside. But everyone knows that kids are poor. Kids never have money, except for maybe a little bit of pocket money. So kids don't feel crappy about not having money, because they've never had any to begin with. It doesn't affect us like it does adults—or teenagers, who are just starting to feel crappy about money.

Meredith said that getting guys off was the best way she knew how to make the most amount of money in the shortest amount of time. That's what Gina had said too, except that she'd said it about dancing. Plus Gina really liked dancing. She was always dancing around the apartment, when we lived in apartments, or in the motel room, when we lived in motel rooms. Sometimes she'd even dance in line at the Tim Horton's if a song came on that she liked. I hated when she did that and one time I left without even getting anything because I was so mad at her for embarrassing me and so mad at the skeezy construction workers behind us who ogled her up and down and whistled and clucked their tongues and said, "Ooh, Mama!" and then I got mad at Gina all over again for letting them do it. Gina had laughed at me and told me I was too serious and that I needed to lighten up. There are times to be serious and there are other times, too. But not everyone agrees on which times are which.

So far, Meredith had been working almost half a year, but she still didn't have enough money to get Steve out of jail.

"What about stealing?" I asked her one day while we ate our Big Macs.

"Like wallets and shit?"

"Yeah."

"Too risky." She picked some polish off her finger nail. "What if they caught me? I don't want to get beaten up. Or get sent to juvie."

"Have you ever?"

"What? Got beaten up?"

"Yeah."

She put down her Big Mac. A little bit of secret sauce oozed out the side of her lip. I pointed to my lip and she wiped hers with the back of her hand. "Tucker?"

"Yeah?"

"I'm going to tell you something."

"Okay." I chose an extra-long fry from my fry-packet and stuck it in the side of my mouth like a cigarette. I watched Meredith as she pulled her hair back into a ponytail and wrapped a purple elastic around it.

"You're the only person who knows what I do and doesn't make me feel like a piece of shit for doing it. You're the only person who doesn't judge me," she said.

"Why would I judge you? It's just a job."

"*See*, that's exactly what I'm talking about."

"Are you going to eat the rest of your fries?"

She handed me her carton of fries.

"Thanks."

"And I know we haven't known each other for very long, but I feel like I can trust you."

"Me too. About you." I smiled at her. The sunlight coming through the window bounced off her eyes, making them look like green beach-glass. If I had pieces in my beach-glass collection that were the colour of Meredith's eyes, they would be my favourite pieces, and I would keep them in my pocket so I could take them out and look at them anytime I wanted. I kept chewing, and stared into her eyes as she spoke.

"A few months ago, before I met you, while I was working, I … um, I was raped."

I let the fries in my mouth fall out onto the tray in a maggoty-white clump.

"So … " she looked out the window.

"Did you call the cops?"

"Yeah, right."

"What?"

"What was I going to say, 'Hi, I'm a prostitute and I was just raped while I was working, will you come help me out please, officer?' They would've laughed and hung up on me."

"But it's illegal."

"It's a workplace hazard, my friend."

"That's the worst thing I've ever heard."

"Well, there's more."

I stared at her.

"The guy who raped me also made me pregnant."

I stared at her.

"I'm pregnant."

I stared at her.

"I'm going to get an abortion tomorrow, and I want to you to come with me."

I stared at her.

"Tucker?"

I stared at her.

"Will you?"

"Okay."

***

Abortion is when a doctor vacuums an unborn baby out of its

mom. Some people think abortion is murdering babies but how can you murder someone who isn't even technically born yet? When we lived in Red Deer, I passed the hospital on my way to school every day and there were always people marching out front with huge signs around their necks. They reminded me of the Playing Cards in *Alice in Wonderland* who try to paint all the white roses red before the Queen of Hearts notices. But instead of spades or diamonds, their cards said things like "Abortion Is Murder!" "God Hates Abortionists!" and "Abortion Stops a Beating Heart." And I never saw any of them painting roses or anything else. I was eight and didn't know what abortion meant at the time, so Gina explained it to me.

"So is it right or wrong?" I asked her.

"Abortion?"

"Yeah."

She sighed, puffing out her lips. "I don't think there's really an answer to that one, cupcake," she said. "It's probably one of those things that people are never really going to agree on."

"Oh." I didn't understand that. Was abortion like an impossible math question that mathematicians could work on solving for their whole lives and still never get the solution to? Like finding all the digits of pi? "Was *I* an abortion?"

"No, honey, you were born."

"Oh. Because Scott Wilcox called me an abortion once."

"Well, that was a really mean thing for him to say to you, and he's not a good friend."

"I know that."

"Okay."

"He's not even my friend."

"That's good. He sounds mean."

"He is!"

"Did you call him a name back?"

"Yes," I said.

"What?"

"Butt-munchkin."

Gina tried not to laugh, but she wasn't doing a very good job of it. "Tucker—"

"Well, he's really short!"

Then Gina cracked up and so did I.

***

When I got back to the group home after school that afternoon, I went upstairs to use the bathroom. Someone had tried to flush a paper towel and then laid a gigantic poop-log on top of it, and the toilet was overflowing and was about to flood the bathroom floor. I had to get out of there fast or else I'd puke. I ran past the staffroom on my way outside and yelled, "Brian! The upstairs toilet exploded!" Then I went and peed behind a bush in the backyard.

After that I went to visit Gina. I had to tell her that I wouldn't be able to come during visiting hours tomorrow. But I hadn't told her about Meredith, and I couldn't tell her about Meredith's abortion appointment because Meredith had made me swear on Gina's grave and my own grave that I would never tell another living soul about it for as long as I lived, cross my heart and hope to die. I don't know why I hadn't told Gina about Meredith yet, I just hadn't. If I didn't tell Gina about her, then Meredith was all mine. She was my secret friend that no one could say anything bad about and no one could take away. Maybe a part of me was scared that Gina wouldn't like me hanging around with a sixteen-year-old, maybe she would think Meredith was too old for me and that I should be hanging around with kids my own age, like the idiot kids in my class who still ate paste and the dope-monkeys who spent all day in the arcade and didn't ever play Ms. Pac-Man and never even came close to getting a top score on anything they *did* play. Anyways, I went to see Gina.

Mrs Jorgenson was yelling about her bowels when I walked in, and I almost spun around on my heel and left. But I didn't. Gina's face lit up like a thousand-watt bulb when she saw me, and she waved me over to her bed. Mrs Jorgenson yelled something at me that wasn't English and then started hacking into her phlegm jar.

"Tucker, I *need* to get out of this room."

"I know."

"I need to breathe fresh air."

"Okay."

"Go get Heather and tell her I need to go outside. Now."

I ran out of the room.

Fifteen minutes later, I was wheeling Gina down the hall and into the elevator. The elevator stopped on the floor below us, and a janitor got on. He had a yellow bucket on wheels with a stringy grey mop in it. He held onto the mop and pressed the button marked B. I stared at the bucket while we went down. I realized that the things he had to mop up weren't normal things like spilled milk and muddy boot-tracks. The things he had to mop up in the hospital were, like, pee and poo and blood, and people's worst messes of their lives. I looked at the janitor. He didn't seem too upset by all the messes. He gave me a quick smile and Gina a nod. Gina smiled up at him like he was some kind of movie star. Maybe she was just happy to be looking at someone other than Mrs Jorgenson for a change.

I took Gina to the cafeteria. We both got soft-serve ice cream in paper cups. Swirl. That's half-chocolate, half-vanilla. Gina says, why have just one flavour when you can have both? After we got our ice cream, I wheeled her outside and she sucked in great big gulps of air like she was trying not to drown.

"This is wonderful! It smells so good out here!"

Actually it smelled like diesel fumes and antiseptic, but I didn't mention it. It smelled delicious compared to Prince George. We ate our ice cream and watched the cars and people and birds. We watched a guy attached to an IV roll out for a smoke.

Gina held up her wooden spoon. "This is one of the best things I've ever eaten!"

"It's pretty good," I said.

"Pretty good? Tucker, it's fantastic!"

I laughed.

"I'm getting another one."

"Okay."

"Do you want one?"

"No thanks."

"All right, can you get me one then?" she gazed up at me, squinting in the sun. "Please?"

"Um, sure." I looked around. Some nurses were smoking, some patients were smoking. The guy attached to his IV clattered back inside. Some old people were putting money in the parking machine. I don't know why, but I felt nervous about leaving Gina alone outside in her wheelchair. What if she rolled into a car? What if someone stole her?

"Tucker?"

Did people steal moms? I knew they stole kids. They probably stole moms, too. Moms would be more useful actually, come to think of it. If you were going to steal a person, you might as well steal a mom. Then she could make you dinner and do your laundry and help you fix your sweaters. A kid would just want to watch TV and eat chips all day.

"Honey?"

"Yeah?"

"Swirl?"

"Okay. Right. Yeah. Stay here. Don't move, okay?"

"Okay ... "

When I came back out, Gina shoved her arm in front of my face, "Look!" An orange lady bug rested below her elbow and above her hospital bracelet. "Isn't she beautiful?"

I smiled. Most people don't like beetles, but everyone loves ladybugs. But ladybugs are really just small beetles. It's not fair.

"Good luck for me," Gina said. Then the ladybug clacked its tiny wings and flew away. We watched it float off in the breeze.

"I've got good news and bad news," I said. "What do you want first?"

"Oh, man. Give me the bad. No, the good. No, wait. The bad. Definitely the bad first."

"Okay. The bad news is, I'm not going to be able to come see you tomorrow during visiting hours."

"Oh." Her eyes shot icicles through my heart. "How come?"

"Now you're ready for the good news?"

"Yes."

"The good news is I'm going to Marineland."

"Really?"

"Yeah, it's like a field trip thing for kids at the group home."

I couldn't remember ever lying to Gina before, and it felt like a thousand punches in the stomach all at once. But I figured lying was one of those things that gets easier the more you do it. That explains why adults can lie all the time without even feeling bad about it, because they've had lots of practice.

"Because I thought we were going to go to Marineland together," Gina said.

"We still can!"

"All right, you're right. We'll go another time."

"Yeah."

"You know I wanted to take you though, right?"

"I know." *You should have taken me when you had the chance instead of going out to look for a stupid job and getting hit by a stupid mini-van,* I thought. But I didn't say it because I knew it was mean. And the one person you should never be mean to is your mom. Sometimes I screw that up, but I try hard to remember.

"But, yeah, you go. Have fun. It'll be fun. Do you need some money?"

"I have some left from what you gave me before."

"Good. That's good." Gina tapped her nails against the arm of her wheelchair. Then she had a coughing fit that was so bad that a nurse who was on her smoke break asked Gina if she was all right. Gina said yes, but the nurse went and got her a little cup of water anyways and eventually Gina quit coughing.

"Sorry," Gina said.

"It's okay," I said. "I think maybe the ice cream was too cold."

"Maybe," she said.

We didn't say anything for some time. An airplane flew over and left a white scar across the face of the sky. But after a while, the sky healed itself, and the white streak dissolved into the blue.

# 9

In the morning, Meredith and I walked to the clinic and stopped for Coke Slurpees on the way. As I watched her fill her cup, all I could think was: *She's pregnant. There's a baby inside her. Right now. Some bad man's baby that's going to get vacuumed out and then ... and then ...* I don't know what happens after that. Meredith wore cut-off jean shorts and a Hypercolor T-shirt that all the colour had drained out of. She knew that we should go around the back of the clinic to avoid the *Alice in Wonderland* people, and I was glad for it. The woman at the front desk raised her eyebrows when we came in together. She gave Meredith a form to fill out and a pen with yellow holographic happy faces on it. We sat beside each other on the hard white chairs. Meredith chewed her nails as she filled out the form. I swung my legs from the chair and looked around at the other women in the waiting room. One wore huge white sunglasses that made her look like an alien. One blew her face off into a Kleenex. One had her face mashed against the chest of a man with the biggest ears I'd ever seen. Were all the women in the waiting room having an abortion? Had they all been raped? The only way to ever know would be to ask each one of them. And *that* is what Ms Snyder, my grade-three teacher in Vancouver, would have called an inappropriate question. I tried not to think about the other people in the waiting room and made up a joke instead.

"Knock knock."

"Who's there?" Meredith spit a piece of her fingernail onto the floor.

"Nana."

"Nana who?"

"Nana your business."

She smiled for a millisecond then turned back to the form.

"Meredith?" the nurse called.

Meredith looked at me and bit her bottom lip.

"Break a leg," I said.

She took a deep breath and followed the nurse down the white hallway.

\*\*\*

She came out about twenty minutes later and we went out into the street. She walked fast, too fast, and I had to jog along beside her to keep up. She didn't say anything so I didn't either. We sat down on a concrete barrier beside the Horseshoe Falls. It was louder than a hundred million jackhammers all going at once. A watery rainbow shimmered in the mist below.

"So?" I said.

"They didn't do it."

"Oh."

"She said it was too late for her to do it." Meredith put her face in her hands.

"Oh."

"I waited too long."

"So, what are you—"

"She gave me the number of a doctor in Toronto who would maybe still do it. But it costs a shitload. And, it would … it would feel it, I guess," Meredith shrugged. "Maybe."

"Did you see it?"

"Yeah."

"What was it like?"

"Like staring into the sun."

"Wow."

I stole a look at her belly. There was a bulge there, but you couldn't really tell if it was a baby or fat. We watched two seagulls swoop and dive beside the waterfall, playing in the mist. A guy rode by us on a BMX. Two old ladies hobbled past us, both of them with silver canes. A man and lady walked past us, and the man had a kangaroo pouch strapped to him with a baby inside. I looked at Meredith. Her bottom lip was bleeding from biting it so hard. She rubbed her eyes. "I don't know what to do," she said.

"Well, if this were a *Choose Your Own Adventure* book, which it isn't, obviously, because it's your life, but if it were, you would have three options. One, have the baby and keep it. Two, have the baby and give it up for adoption. Or three, have an abortion. But whichever one you pick, you'll have to go to that next page no matter what. You can't cheat and turn back and choose a different one."

"There's a fourth option."

"There is? What?"

"Take a flying leap off the falls."

"That's not a good option," I said.

"Why not?"

"At least stuff yourself into a barrel first."

She looked at me for a second, then burst out laughing.

"And if you wait until you're *really* pregnant then you can have, like, a built-in airbag in there with you."

We laughed until she began to cry. She made tiny, chipmunk sounds as she cried. I put my arm around her shoulder and she let me. Then I rubbed little circles into her back like Gina did for me whenever I cried. It didn't help. She cried even harder. I stared at her hair. Mist clung to it like tiny diamonds. I wished I could help her, but I couldn't do anything. I was only a kid, like her.

"I saw this sign in front of St. Ann's church the other day," I said. "It was a good one. I wanted to remember it."

"What did it say?" She looked up. Her tears had streaked her makeup and left black ribbons around her eyes.

"All shall be well, and all shall be well, and all manner of things shall be well."

She nodded and reached into her bag for her cigarettes.

\*\*\*

The next day, Brian, Meredith, and I sat out on the front porch. We were outside because Shawn, Josh, and Kyle were having a farting contest in the kitchen and the whole house reeked. They refused to open any windows or turn on the fan because they said it would skew the results of the contest. Besides, it was one of our first real spring days with sunshine and robins and everything, and it felt good to be outside. Brian tuned his guitar, Meredith read *Watership Down*, and I looked at a ladybug under a magnifying glass. It was orange, not red, and had six spots. I'm not sure if it was a girl or a boy. Not all ladybugs are girls. Some people say the number of spots they have is how old they are, but that could be a myth. People make up stuff that's not true all the time just to sound smart, and then other people who want to sound smart repeat what they said. That's how false information gets spread around. And myths. And urban legends. The people who know they're making stuff up are worse than the people who say it and think it's actually true. We call the people who make stuff up bullshitters. Gina says the world is full of bullshitters, and our job is to see through them. That doesn't mean using X-ray vision; it means being able to tell when people are making stuff up that's not true. I figured the ladybug was probably only a few months old, maybe a year, tops, but definitely not six. I was pretty sure it wasn't the same one that had landed on Gina's arm.

"Hey! What are you doing?" Meredith yelled at me.

"I'm just looking at it."

"Don't do that!"

"Why not?"

"You'll kill it! The sun will zap it through the glass."

I looked at Brian.

"It could," he shrugged.

"It will! It'll incinerate her!"

"How do you know it's a her?"

"JUST—"

"Okay, okay." I put the magnifying glass in my pocket.

Meredith whipped her book across the lawn.

"Careful," Brian said.

"That book is stupid. Most of it isn't even in English."

"So the rabbits have their own language, what's wrong with that?" Brian said.

"I can't understand it is what's wrong with that!" Meredith shouted.

Brian scratched his beard. "How about I play a song for you guys?"

"Okay," I said.

Meredith grumbled and adjusted herself until she sat cross-legged in the green plastic lawn chair. She picked at her elbow and said, "Whatever."

"Okay." Brian cleared his throat and began to play his guitar and sing. It was Nirvana.

Meredith closed her eyes and leaned back in her chair. I watched the wind ripple through the grass and felt an invisible chicken bone stuck in my throat. I didn't want to be at Bright Light Youth Residence anymore. I wanted to go home. That's not a house that I grew up in in a town that I can always go back to. That's not the Niagara Motel with Chad the front-desk guy with the scorpion tattoo on his neck and

Chloe's earring behind the sink in our room. That's Gina.

I don't usually get all sentimental like that, but then I realized why I was. It was like a Jedi Mind Trick that Brian was doing with his song. I knew that song from before. Gina had played it at our apartment in Medicine Hat, in her room late at night when she smoked cigarettes out her window and thought she was getting away with it. She had played it in the kitchenette of our room in Prince George on our yellow ghettoblaster while she made me grilled cheese and pickles for lunch. The song was why I'd thought of her, the song was what was making my throat lump up. I guess because:

1. I wasn't with her, and

2. Because I didn't know when or if she would be okay again.

It seemed to me that Gina would either get better or die, and I wasn't sure which one was going to happen. But I did know there was no way I could live at Bright Light for the next eight years of my life.

Brian finished the song with a little flourish of his fingers. He put the pick in his mouth while he twisted the white knobs on the end of the guitar. Brian's pick was sky blue. The real name for a pick is plectrum, pick is just a short form. Brian taught me that. Brian was actually a really nice guy. He'd let us watch TV past nine p.m., which none of the other SODs did. He shared his wine gums with me and he always saved me the black ones because he knew they were my favourite. Brian was in a band called Wax Wings. I'd never seen them live because they played at bars and clubs that only adults can get into, but their demo tape was at the house and I'd heard Meredith playing it a katrillion times. They weren't the worst band I'd ever heard, but they weren't the best either. Meredith stared at Brian.

"Do you really think you're going to make it?" she said. Her face was all shiny and pink.

"What do you mean?" He took the pick out of his mouth.

"I mean as a musician. You think you're going to get famous? Get played on the radio?"

"Well, I don't know for sure, but I have to try, right?"

"Why?" she asked.

"Why what?"

"Why do you have to try?"

He played a few chords. "Because then I'll know that I did everything I could, and I won't have to wonder."

"But won't you be so disappointed if it doesn't work out?"

"Yeah, I guess," he nodded. "But there are worse things than being disappointed."

Meredith wore a little half-smile. I stared past her and watched a crow hop around on the telephone wire in front of the house. It was okay for people to talk about the future being full of possibility and the future holding good things for them, because the truth is, the future never comes.

I went inside to make a peanut butter and pickle sandwich. While I was making it, I heard yelling coming from the TV room. Kyle and Shawn were playing foosball and wouldn't let Dirtbag Daryl play.

"Don't touch it, shitbucket," Kyle said.

"I can play if I want," Daryl said.

"No," Shawn said. "You can't."

"Why not?"

"Because I'm going to bash your face in with my boot if you come within three feet of this table while we're playing. Now, fuck off, Dirtbag."

I got a glass of milk because milk makes a body good and went into the TV room and sat on the couch to eat my sandwich and watch *The Fresh Prince of Bel-Air*.

"Hey, I've got something for you guys," Daryl said, pulling a crumpled pack of Export A's out of his pocket.

"Where'd you get those?" Kyle grabbed for the pack.

"Ah-ah! Not so fast. Only if you let me play."

"Sure, you can play," Shawn said, nodding to Kyle.

"Really?"

In one quick movement, Kyle had Dirtbag Daryl's arms pinned behind his back. Kyle tossed the cigarettes to Shawn and Shawn laughed as he took one out and tucked it behind his ear. "Yeah, play with yourself, wanker."

"You fuck-off! Those are mine! Give them back!" Daryl screamed. "They're not yours!"

"They are now, you dumb shit." Shawn put the pack in his pocket.

Brian and Meredith came into the room then, probably to see what all the noise was about. I looked at Dirtbag Daryl. His back was to me and he was hunched over a little, and he seemed to be vibrating, which was not unusual for Dirtbag Daryl. What happened next was in slow motion. Daryl soared toward Shawn with the blade of his Swiss Army knife open. "I'll cut you! I'll cut you, you asshole!" Shawn put his palms up as Daryl held the knife to Shawn's eye. Brian put his hand on Daryl's shoulder and Daryl spun around and plunged the knife into Brian's neck. I let my sandwich fall to the floor. Kyle, Shawn, Daryl, Meredith, and I stared at Brian as his hands flew to his neck, his blood spraying the walls. The colour drained from his face and he opened his mouth. No words came out, only a red bubble. Then he collapsed.

I think I screamed. I'm not sure. Maybe we all did. I remember looking at Meredith, her mouth forming a perfect little *o*. I'd like to say we took swift action and immediately called 9-1-1, but the truth is, we all just stood there, mesmerized, as Brian's blood gushed from his neck like a broken fire-hydrant, forming a dark puddle around him. It was exactly like a movie, except that it was real. That was the worst part. It was all real. Brian stared up at the water-stained ceiling, his brown eyes shiny with tears.

I was shaking. I wanted to throw up. I don't remember sitting down, but suddenly I was on the floor.

It was Daryl who finally called 9-1-1, crying, apologizing to all of us, to Brian, to the 9-1-1 operator, to God.

All of us kids stood at the front window and watched in silence as the paramedics covered Brian with a white sheet, loaded him onto a stretcher, and rolled him into the ambulance. They did not turn the sirens on. That was the worst. That they didn't even turn them on. We all had our arms wrapped around ourselves as we watched Brian being taken away, as if we could somehow hold the sadness in, if we just held on tight enough. We watched as Daryl, head bowed, was pushed into the back of the police cruiser, turning his face away from us and toward some unknown future. The cherry lights on top of the police cruiser sparkled against the clear blue sky as they drove away.

# 10

Things were pretty miserable at Bright Light after that. A butt-load of reporters came to the house to get us kids on camera saying how shocking and awful it all was. Of course I wanted to be on TV, but not for that. Not for something like that. When the pretty TV reporter asked me what I thought about the recent stabbing, I said, "It was the worst thing I've ever seen."

"Would you care to elaborate for us?" she asked, shoving the microphone in my face.

"No," I said. Then I went upstairs to the boys' dorm and tried not to look at Dirtbag Daryl's bunk on the way by. I sat on my bed and threw my red super-bounce against the wall about a hundred-thousand times until I was sure all the reporters had left, then I went downstairs and made myself a bacon and peanut butter sandwich with some leftover bacon I found in the fridge. But then I remembered that Brian had made that bacon for us, just the day before, and I wasn't hungry at all anymore, so I threw the sandwich in the garbage.

That day and the day after, two police officers came. One man and one woman. The woman had freckles and short blonde hair, and the man was built like a warthog and had a shaved head. They spoke to each of us inside the staff room, which was really just an office with a messy desk, a grey metal filing cabinet, a mini-fridge, and a bookshelf full of child psychology books. There was a poster on the wall with a lighthouse shining out to the ocean. *RISK* was at the top in big letters and below the lighthouse it read, *The greater the adversity, the brighter the light of opportunity*. I'm not really sure what that was supposed to mean, but I figured it was probably a secret-coded message to the SODs to not give up on us kids no matter how screwed up we were because we might turn out all right eventually. But when

Brian put his hand on Dirtbag Daryl's shoulder that was a risk, and look where it got him. The lady-cop asked me my name and how old I was and if I had seen what happened that day. While I answered her, I read the other poster behind the desk. It was of a space shuttle taking off with lots of smoke below it. At the top it read, *TEAMWORK*. Below the picture of the rocket it read, *Teamwork is the fuel that allows people to work together toward a common vision. It is the fuel that allows common people to attain uncommon results.* Then I started to wonder who these common people were. Were Gina and I common people? Was Brian? Was everyone except astronauts? I didn't really know what that poster meant either, but I liked the picture of the rocket so I focused on that and tried not to cry in front of the police officers. The lady-cop asked me to tell them in my own words what had happened. I thought that was a stupid thing for her to say because who else's words would I use but my own? Anyways, I stared at the rocket ship and told them what I'd seen. I told them what I thought: that it was an accident and I was ninety-nine-percent sure that Dirtbag Daryl hadn't planned it. I was a hundred-percent sure he didn't mean to kill Brian. I knew that for a fact because of the way he cried afterwards, because of the way he dialed 9-1-1, and how his voice got when he spoke to the operator. And to us. It was just one of those awful things. One of those split-second things that ruins people's lives forever.

"Everyone makes mistakes," my voiced cracked as I said it.

"That's true, Tucker," the man-cop said. "But most people's mistakes don't end in a fatality."

I stared at the rocket ship and wished I was on it. Going far, far away from Earth and all the terrible mistakes that everyone on it makes every day. I wished I was going someplace peaceful like the moon or Mars, which they say is the planet of war, except that Mars is probably a kajillion times more peaceful than Earth.

\*\*\*

The next day, a grief counsellor came to speak to us. Everybody cried a lot. Not just girls, boys too. Meredith was really upset. I think she might have been in love with Brian. I know she really missed him. We all did.

The grief counsellor's name was Amy. Amy wore turquoise hoop earrings and a lot of mascara. She talked to us as a group and then individually. We talked in the SOD office. She wanted to know how I was feeling.

"I don't know," I said.

"You can be feeling more than one thing," she said.

"I know that."

"Okay."

I cleared my throat. "I just ... miss him. And Daryl too, I guess."

She jotted a small note on her yellow legal pad. "What else?" she smiled.

"I ... I want to go home."

Amy nodded and squished her lips together. "Where's home, Tucker?"

I shrugged. "The Niagara Motel, I guess."

Amy wrote that down on her pad.

After that I went up to the boys' dorm. No one was in there so I took out my box of special stuff and got my little dog Charlie out and put him on my pillow. I lay down next to him and petted him a little bit and told him that everything would be okay, that he shouldn't worry, that he was a good dog, a good boy. A while later, Shawn came into the room, and I tucked Charlie under my pillow so he wouldn't see him, and, for the zillionth time, I wished that I had a real dog.

# 11

About a week after that, I sat on the outdoor couch with Meredith. It was that time after the day is over but before night has come, when the sky is sort of purply-grey and everything moves slower. We both had blankets over us. Not because it was cold out but because sometimes blankets can make you feel like everything's okay, even when you know it's not.

"I can't do it," Meredith said.

I looked over at her.

"I thought I could. I wanted to, but now I just know I can't."

I nodded.

"In the same way that you know you'll never kick an animal." She lit a cigarette and took a big sigh as she exhaled.

"Maybe if it's a boy, you could name him Brian," I said.

She wiped away a tear that had leaked out the side of her eye.

Car tires screeched a few blocks away. The group home was dark behind us, but we could hear someone crying in the downstairs bathroom. Whoever it was sounded like a wailing puppy.

"I need to get out of here," Meredith said. "I need a vacation."

"Yeah."

"Even if it's just for a little while, a weekend even."

"That sounds nice," I said.

"Where would you go if you could go anywhere?" Meredith asked, curling into the corner of the couch.

"Boston."

"Why Boston?"

"Because I need to go to the *Cheers* bar."

"Why?"

"To find my real father."

Meredith raised an eyebrow and took a hard drag.

Since by this time, Meredith was pretty much my best friend, I told her about Sam Malone. At first she laughed and told me I was insane, but then I explained to her the very good reasons I had for believing that Sam Malone *could* be my actual father, and if I could just see him, just meet him, just once, I would know.

She said, "Yeah, and my real dad is probably MacGyver because I have a Swiss Army knife and so does he."

I picked at a scab on my elbow.

"Haven't you ever asked your mom about your father?" she said.

"Of course! All the time!"

"And?"

"And nothing. She won't tell me diddly-squat. All I know is what I told you. Brown hair. Bartender. Recovering alcoholic. Womanizer. That's it."

"Does your mom work around a lot of guys in show biz?"

"She works around a lot of guys, period."

"I guess it could be him." Meredith shrugged. "It could be anyone."

"Plus, our last name is Malone."

"But that's not—"

"But it's a pretty big coincidence, don't you think?"

Meredith rolled her eyes, took a slow drag off her cigarette. "All right. So?"

"So, what?"

"So, you want to go to Boston?"

"Yeah!" I jumped off the couch and leapt into the air.

Meredith laughed. It was the first time I'd heard her laugh since before Brian was killed. It was a good sound. "All right, let's go then," she said.

"Really?"

"Yeah. Let's do it."

"For real?

"You've got some money, don't you?" she asked.

"A little bit."

"But you could get more, right?"

"Probably," I said.

She nodded and tapped the ash off her cigarette. "That's what I thought," she said.

***

I hadn't told Gina about Brian getting stabbed which was hard because I don't usually keep secrets from Gina, but I knew that it was a terrible thing to have happened and that it would make her worry and make her upset and then her heart wouldn't heal properly. Heather, the nice nurse, knew about it because she'd seen it on the news, but I knew that Gina hadn't or else she would've mentioned it already.

The next time I saw Heather, she gave me a Long John. I knew they were her favourite so I asked her if she was sure. She said they were actually her second-favourite after Hawaiian donuts and also that I needed it more than she did.

"How are you holding up, kid?" she asked.

"I don't know. Okay, I guess."

"That's good, that's good," she nodded.

"But, listen, Gina can't find out, okay? It will make her worry too much, and then, you know—"

"She won't hear it from me," Heather said.

"Thanks."

Then Heather hugged me. She had big pillowy boobs the size of couch cushions and it was really nice because she was so warm and big around me that I felt like I could almost disappear right into her. Fat people give the best hugs.

After that, Heather went back to the nurses' station and I went to see Gina. I knew that I had to tell Gina I was going away for a little while because she would wonder why I wasn't coming to visit her and then she'd get super-worried and that would be super-bad. So after Meredith and I figured out all the details of the plan to go to Boston, and I believed it was really going to happen and wasn't just one of those things that people *talk* about doing but never actually *do*, I went to see Gina. It was a P.A. day, which meant I didn't have to go to school, but I skipped watching cartoons and eating cereal in my pyjamas and instead got dressed and went straight to the hospital.

Mrs Jorgensen wasn't in her bed, which was made up all tight and neat. Gina held her arms open, and I ran to her and hugged her. She smiled and kissed me on top of my head and smelled my hair.

"Where's Mrs Jorgensen?"

Gina patted the side of her bed, and I scooted down to where I could sit without hurting her. "She didn't make it, lovey."

"Didn't make what?"

"She passed."

"She *died?*"

Gina nodded.

"Holy crap." I looked over at Mrs Jorgensen's bed. She had only ever yelled at us and coughed and hacked and spat wads of phlegm into her little glass jar, but it didn't seem right that she wasn't there anymore, that she would never do any of those things again.

"I think I miss her," I whispered.

"I think I do too," Gina said.

Then I carefully lay down next to Gina so that I wasn't touching her broken ribs. She smoothed my hair, and I turned my face away from her and let hot tears spill out onto the green sheets. Gina stroked my hair, and after a while I fell asleep and when I woke up again, my eyes were sticky with eye-crusties and hard to open. I rinsed my face in the sink in Gina's little bathroom and then we watched *Family Feud*. The one family was sort of stupid, and none of them guessed the right answers to anything, and the other family was super-smart and were probably all doctors and lawyers and scientists, so it didn't really seem fair. But no one gets to choose their family. The best you can hope for is that they don't forget about you when it's your turn in the Isolation Booth. After *Family Feud*, *The Golden Girls* came on. We watched it for a bit, but then Gina didn't want to watch it anymore because she said Sophia reminded her of Mrs Jorgensen and she was getting sad so we went down to the cafeteria to get hot chocolates with whipped-cream on top. Gina wanted to go outside, but it was raining and I didn't want her to get all wet and cold, so I said no deal.

"Tucker, come on, take me outside. I want a cigarette." She pulled a crumpled pack from her purse.

"Where did you get those?"

"Mrs Jorgensen."

"She gave them to you?"

"Not exactly."

"You *stole* them? You stole cigarettes from a dead lady?"

"Shh, calm down. They were just going to throw them out anyways. And besides, she would've wanted me to have them." Gina pulled a cigarette from the pack and tapped it against the box. "Please take me outside." She rocked back and forth in her wheelchair so that it rolled a little bit forward.

"Gina, you have a collapsed lung. Do you really think you should be smoking?"

"Look, it's just something I have to do, okay? When someone dies, you smoke a cigarette. You think of them and blow the smoke up to guide them on their journey. It's a tradition."

"Whatever you say, boss."

"Don't get smart."

"Can't help it," I said, and rolled her outside.

"And don't you dare tell Dr Chopra. She'll be livid."

Gina smoked and we listened to the rain. "Here," she said, holding out the cigarette to me. "Take a little puff. Not too big."

I did and coughed a lot so she would think I'd never smoked before. I handed it back to her. "So I won't be able to come visit you this weekend," I said, feeling my heart speed up.

"Why not?"

"My friend from the group home invited me to her family reunion. And it's in Toronto. It's at her uncle's place and he has an indoor swimming pool and a hot tub, and she has lots of cousins my age and everyone's staying for the whole weekend. I really want to go. Please, can I? *Please?*" It felt weird and wrong lying to Gina, but, just like I thought, it got a little bit easier every time I did it.

Gina sighed. "What's your friend's name?"

"Mary." I don't know why I said that, it just came out.

"How old is Mary?"

"My age."

Gina looked at me with her squishy face. "Is Mary your girlfriend?"

"*Ew!* No! Come *on*, Gina! She's just my *friend* who's a *girl!*"

"Okay, okay. Take it easy."

"So, anyways. Can I?"

"How are you going to get to Toronto?"

"Her aunt is going to drive us."

"Both ways?"

"Yep."

"Will you call me every day and let me know you're okay?"

"Yep."

"You promise?"

"Promise."

"Pinky swear," she said, and held up her pinky.

We pinky swore, and I made a mental note to remember to take the number of the hospital with me so I could call her. A mental note is not actually written out on paper like a real note. It's a note that you write just to yourself on the walls of your own brain.

"Want another hot chocolate?" she asked, tossing her cigarette into the gutter.

"Yeah."

"Me too."

I wheeled her back to the cafeteria.

"Do I have to sign anything?" she asked.

"For what?"

"For the group home. So they know you have my permission to go with Mary for the weekend?"

"Um, I don't think so. I'll ask."

"Okay." She squinted at me.

A herd of wild horses galloped through my chest. My tongue throbbed. She knew I was lying, she knew everything. It was all over.

Then an old guy with red spots the size of coins all over his face hobbled past us. "There's a sight for sore eyes!" he said and winked at Gina.

"Hi, Mr Hanson." She gave him a little wave.

"Is that your new boyfriend?" he said, pointing to me. "You cheating on me?"

"This is my son, Tucker. Tucker, this is Mr Hanson." Gina smiled.

Mr Hanson and I shook hands. His hand was cold and felt like a paper bag.

"Good-looking fella. Wonder where he gets that from?" He winked at Gina again. "I'm on a hunt for rice pudding. See you folks later."

Gina and I had a little laugh after he left. Not that we were laughing at him, at least I don't think we were. Maybe just a little bit. But not in a mean way. You can laugh *at* people and you can laugh *with* people, and sometimes you can do both at the same time. We finished our hot chocolates, and I got up to get us some water. When I came back to the table, Gina was picking at her nails. I sat down across from her and took a big drink from my water. She looked up at me and gave me a small smile, then went back to her nails.

"Gina, are we white trash?"

"No!"

"Poor white trash?"

"*No!* Who told you that?"

"No one. I was just wondering."

"We're not poor, Tucker."

"Okay."

"We're thrifty."

"Oh."

"And it's not your job to worry about money. It's mine."

I nodded.

"Do you need some spending money for Toronto?"

I nodded.

She took her wallet out of her purse and found her bank card. She passed it across the table to me. "Go down to the Bank of Nova Scotia and use the machine to take out some money. There should be some left in the savings account."

"Okay."

"You know the password?"

"Open sesame?"

"No, silly."

I laughed.

"It's the year of your birth," she whispered.

"1981?"

"That's right."

"Okay."

"Okay?"

"Yeah. Thanks, Gina."

"Tucker, you're not white trash. You never have been and you never will be. And I don't want you associating with anyone who would call you that."

"Okay."

"Got it?"

"Got it."

"Good."

I drank the rest of my water and tried not to look at Gina. I hid my grin in my glass. I was going to Boston.

# 12

Meredith could borrow a car for a few days from this guy who she said owed her a favour. Apparently he was good friends with her brother, Steve. Not good enough friends to bail him out, though. The big coincidence was that the guy who owed Meredith a favour was Chad, the front-desk guy with the scorpion tattoo from the Niagara Motel. So I got to ride in Chad's black Chevrolet Caprice again. I had taken $300 out of Gina's savings account to add to the $96.50 I still had left over from what she gave me before. Meredith had taken it all to the bank and changed it into US dollars for me and got some of her own money changed too. We left Niagara Falls a little after five a.m. We wanted to get an early start so all the kids would still be asleep as well as the SOD that night, Paula. I had packed my backpack the night before and gone to bed with my clothes on. I took all of my stuff with me, just in case. Gina always says it's better to have it and not need it than to need it and not have it.

As I opened the door of the boys' dorm to leave, Josh rolled over. A bar of light leaking in from the hallway fell across his face. His eyes were open and he looked at me. I held my breath and nodded, once. Then he closed his eyes and rolled back toward the wall. I held my breath all the way down the hall and all the way down the stairs. I held it as I unbolted and unchained the locks on the front door. I held it until I closed the door behind me and was outside.

Meredith was waiting for me on the porch. She smiled and I smiled back, and we both looked up at the windows to see if anyone had turned a light on. No one had. Meredith put a finger to her lips and we tiptoed down the steps and ran across the street and into the alley. We took the alley up to the Niagara Motel where we found

Chad's Caprice parked around back by the dumpsters.

"You sure you want to do this?" Meredith jingled the keys around her finger.

"Yep. Are you?"

"Definitely. I'm so glad to be out of that shithole."

"Me too," I said. I hoped I could find Sam Malone and stay with him until Gina got better, and then I wouldn't ever have to go back to Bright Light. Of all the crappy places I've lived, it was definitely the worst. As Kyle and Shawn would've said, it was the suckiest bunch of sucks that ever sucked.

Meredith threw me the keys. "You drive."

"Um, I'm not—"

"*Psych!*"

Chad's car smelled like cigarette butts and the green leaf air-freshener. About five minutes after we started to drive, Meredith ripped the air-freshener off the rear-view mirror and threw it out the window. She said that the smell of it would make her puke. About two minutes after that she pulled over, opened her door, and then, she *did* puke.

"Are you okay?" I said.

"No, I'm pregnant," she said. She spat on the ground then closed her door. She wiped her mouth on the back of her hand. "Did you bring any water?"

I handed her my water and tried not to think about her gross puke-germs getting on my water bottle. Then I remembered about AIDS and got nervous. I wondered if you could get AIDS from sharing drinks, and I wondered if Meredith had it. I hoped not. People who get AIDS don't ever get better and there's nothing anyone can do to help them, no matter how much money they have or how good at basketball they are. Meredith drank half the bottle, then handed it back to me and started the car. I wiped it off with my T-shirt and put it in my backpack. The sun was rising as we drove over the Rainbow Bridge, and the light made a zillion rainbows in the mist of the waterfalls.

We got in line at the border crossing and my heart wobbled. I drummed my fingers against my knees.

"Just let me do the talking," Meredith said.

"Okay."

"Unless they ask you something directly, then you should answer."

"All right."

"Do you have ID?" she said.

"No. Should I?"

She shrugged and moved the car forward until we were at the window of the guard's booth. The border-crossing guard had a dark moustache and tinted brown glasses. His shoulder muscles were as big as my head, and even though he was sitting down, I could tell he was tall.

"Good morning," Meredith said, passing him her driver's license.

"'Morning," he said. "Where are you all off to today?"

"Just going into Buffalo for some shopping," Meredith said. "Wanted to get an early start."

The guard bent his head to peer in at me. "Who's this?"

"This is my kid brother, Jack," Meredith said.

"Hi," I said. I was Jack. I was her brother. I figured *hi* was something Meredith's kid brother Jack would probably say.

"How long do you two plan on staying in the United States?"

"Oh, just for the day. We have to be home by five to help with dinner," she smiled.

"Are you bringing anything into the US today? Any drugs, weapons?"

My hand closed around the Swiss Army knife inside my pocket and I stared straight ahead.

"No," Meredith said. "Just ourselves."

"How much money are you bringing into the US today?"

"About four hundred dollars," she said. "We have to get some new clothes. And shoes."

He eyed our clothes and then his eyes darted around the car. After a few seconds he nodded. "All right, you kids be safe now." He handed Meredith her license back and waved us through.

The gate went up and Meredith pushed the gas, and just like that, we were in a whole other country.

"*Jack?*" I said.

"New Jack City!"

I laughed.

"Welcome to New York State, my friend."

PART TWO

LIVING THE DREAM

# 13

Meredith wouldn't let me touch the radio. She said only the driver gets to pick the music—and the volume also. She switched the radio station every few seconds. She never stayed on one station long enough to even hear the song. I'm not sure she even wanted to listen to music, maybe she just wanted to scan. Finally, "Smells Like Teen Spirit" came on, and she left it on that station. It was Kiss FM, a Buffalo station that played dance hits and some alternative. Gina and I had listened to it before. You can get US radio stations in Canada, but you can't get Canadian stations in the US. I don't know why. Maybe Americans don't like our music and they put up invisible walls that block all the radio waves coming from Canada. But no one knows that the Americans are doing that because the walls are invisible. That would be what's called a conspiracy. Most people think that people who have conspiracy theories are crazy, but it's not always true. And besides, even crazy people can be right about things when nobody else is.

There was a guy named Jake who lived down the hall from me and Gina at the Aladdin Motor Inn, our motel in Red Deer. There were always empty bottles of Alberta Pure Vodka and half-eaten cans of alphabet soup outside Jake's door. Everyone said that Jake was crazy because he always talked about how he'd been abducted by aliens when he was a kid and how they did all kinds of tests on him, and that's why he always beeps when he goes through metal detectors now. Gina said Jake was a liar and not to listen to him, but I don't know why anyone would lie about being abducted by aliens. Plus no one really knows for sure if aliens exist or not, so I didn't think it was really fair to call Jake a liar. One day, Jake and I were sitting on the bench outside the motel, watching the traffic whiz by.

He smoked a cigarette and I played with a blue and red yo-yo that was supposed to light up but never did.

"Jake?"

"Yeah, kid?"

"What did the aliens look like? That took you."

"They were tall and leggy and had wrinkled bluish-grey skin," he said. "Like elephant skin. Black eyes as big as your head."

"And they only took you the one time, they never came back?"

"As far as I know," he said, flicking his cigarette butt into the road.

"Do you think they'll come and take you again?"

"I don't know," Jake said. "I hope so."

"But why would you want them take you again? Weren't they scary?"

Jake shrugged. "Not as scary as people."

We didn't live in Red Deer for very long, and I didn't know Jake very well, but I still think of him sometimes when I see those satellites sail across the night sky, I think of him. And I wonder if he's still at the Aladdin Motor Inn, drinking vodka and eating cold alphabet soup and waiting for the aliens to come back for him.

\*\*\*

Sometimes Meredith didn't want to listen to music at all, she only wanted quiet. Because she was the driver, she also got to decide when and where we would stop. And she always had to pee. She probably stopped to pee about 200 times on the way to Boston. We had to stop so much for Meredith to pee that I was afraid we wouldn't get to the *Cheers* bar before last call and then Sam wouldn't be there. As I waited in the car for Meredith at a Mobil station in Utica, I traced my finger along how much further we had to go on the map and started to get panicky. What if we didn't make it? What if I *never* met Sam Malone? What if I never found my real father? But then I looked up and the sun was still high and bright in the sky and there were nice puffy cumulus clouds with no rain or storm clouds anywhere and then Meredith got back in from the gas station and threw me a Coke and a Snickers bar. She started the car and a good song came on the radio and I put the map away and ate the Snickers and drank the Coke and the spring sun was warm on our faces through the windshield and I felt better. I was going to Boston with my new best friend to meet the man who was probably my father. It could turn out to be the best day of my whole entire life.

Meredith went about six miles over the speed limit, which she said wasn't actually speeding. She said the cops couldn't bust you until you went seven or eight over.

"My brother taught me that," she said.

"Yeah, but isn't he in jail?"

"Yeah, but not for speeding."

Meredith stopped three times to eat. I'm usually always hungry but I could hardly eat anything that day, I was too excited to meet Sam. When we went through the McDonald's drive-through in Schenectady, Meredith asked me if I had any cash and I handed her a ten.

I had 376 American dollars stuffed in a sock at the bottom of my backpack and a twenty-dollar bill in my pocket. It was more cash than I'd ever had at one time. I could buy anything, go anywhere.

"You know that expression, the world is your oyster?" I said.

"Yeah."

"Well, what if you hate seafood? Then it doesn't really make sense, right?"

Meredith eyed me as she drank from her milkshake.

"Could I say, for example, the world is my cheeseburger?"

Meredith shrugged, "I don't see why not."

"The world is my cheeseburger."

She laughed. "*Our* cheeseburger."

"The world is our cheeseburger." I smiled at her and took a big gulp from my milkshake.

"You're a nut, you know that, right?"

\*\*\*

When we finally arrived in Boston, it was already late afternoon. It was raining, but that's springtime for you. It was a nice looking city, and I could see why Sam would want to live there.

"So what's the address?" Meredith asked.

"I don't know."

"You don't have an address?"

"Someone will know where it is. It's famous!"

"Well, who are we going to ask?"

"I don't know, anybody."

"Anybody?"

"Anybody will know. It's frigging *Cheers*, Meredith."

"How about that guy?" she pointed to a man pushing a shopping cart full of bottles and cans. "Do you think he'd know?"

"He might."

Meredith pulled up to him as he clattered down the sidewalk. "Roll your window down."

"But it's pouring rain," I said.

"Well how the hell else do you think we're going to ask him where it is, dick-cheese? Telepathy? Now roll it!"

I rolled my window down and leaned out. "Excuse me," I called. Raindrops splattered against my cheeks.

The man either didn't hear me or didn't care. He didn't look at me, just stared ahead and kept the same pace, the cans and bottles in his cart clanking along.

Meredith drove up to the curb beside him. "Try again," she hissed.

"Um, hello?" I called, louder this time.

The man, still staring straight ahead, gripped the handle of his shopping cart and took off running down the sidewalk.

"Never mind," Meredith said. "He probably didn't know anyways. Ask her." She pointed to a lady with a hot-pink umbrella who was coming out of a hair salon called Krafty Kuts.

"Excuse me? Would you happen to know where the *Cheers* bar is?"

Her dark eyes flickered over us and she shook her head, then hurried away.

Meredith sighed and pulled the car away from the curb.

"I know who will know," I said.

"Who?"

"A cabbie. Cabbies know everything."

"You're right. Let's find a taxi."

"A big yellow taxi," I said.

Meredith rolled her eyes and said, "Beggars can't be choosers," which means, when you need something real bad, you can't be too picky about it. She meant me. I was the beggar. The something I needed real bad was Sam Malone.

We ended up flagging down a white taxi that said White Knight Cab Co. and had a black silhouette of a horse on the side. The driver was really old, probably forty. When I asked him about the Cheers bar, his face crinkled up, and I was afraid that he didn't know where it was and my heart clenched in my chest. But then he grinned and told us exactly how to get there. "Good luck," he said. We got out, and he sped away, spraying a puddle across my jeans.

Finally, after a zillion years, we made it to Beacon Street. From the outside, it looked exactly like it does in the show's opening credits. There was even the sign with the hand pointing down the stairs that said *Cheers Est. 1895*. But I had seen the episode where Sam tells Rebecca that he actually made up that date, so I laughed a little bit to see it there in real-life, because I knew it was fake. Two huge flags fluttered above the bar, an American flag and a yellow and blue one that said *Cheers*. My heart was flapping so hard in my chest by then I wondered if it would fly right out of my body like a bird. I was about to meet Sam Malone. I was about to meet the person who was very likely my father. I squealed a little bit and Meredith made fun of me for sounding like a pig, and then I laughed because it *did* sound like a pig, and then we went down the stairs and I opened the door for Meredith and we went inside.

As soon as I got inside, I knew something was wrong. It was all wrong. The bar wasn't where it was supposed to be and neither were the tables, lamps, and everything else. It was carpeted. It was a completely different colour. It was the wrong bar. My arms felt loose in their sockets. I was afraid I might fall down like Gina sometimes does when she gets a cataplectic attack. I held on tight to the railing and stayed where I was. I looked at Meredith.

"All right, let's go ask the bartender where he is," she said.

The bar's interior didn't seem to be phasing her. I held on to the railing. Meredith started for the bar. I hesitated for a second, then she glanced back at me and I followed her.

"There's Norm," Meredith whispered and pointed to a fat guy sitting in the corner. He scowled at us. It wasn't Norm, though. It wasn't him at all. The bartender had a white moustache, a navy baseball cap, and glasses. He was not Sam and looked nothing like him. If you could take everything that Sam Malone was not and stuff it into a human body, you'd get this guy.

"Hi," Meredith said.

"Good afternoon," he said. His voice was cigarette stained and sounded nothing like Sam's. The song playing over the speakers above us was "Whiter Shade of Pale." I knew that song because Gina liked it and sometimes sang it to me for bedtimes. I wanted to cry. I bit the inside of my cheek really hard instead.

Meredith ordered two Cokes.

"I'm sorry, but we can't serve children in this establishment," the bartender said.

"There's no alcohol in Coke, in case you didn't know that," Meredith said.

"I do know that," he said, and his eyes sparkled behind his glasses.

Meredith elbowed me in the ribs.

"Hi," I said.

"Hi," he said.

"We're looking for Sam Malone. You know, Sam. Sammy."

"From the show," he said.

"Yeah."

"Well, *Cheers* is not filmed here as you probably noticed," he gestured to the room. "And Sam does not work here."

"Well, do you know where he is, then?" I said.

"Right now?" the bartender shrugged. "If I had to wager a guess, I'd say he's probably where most stars are, in Hollywood."

"California?"

"Yeah, I'd say."

"But how do you know that?"

"I know that *Cheers* is filmed at Paramount Pictures in Hollywood, and if Ted Danson's working right now, which he probably is, then he'd be on set."

I barely heard what he said. My head was a flurry and the inside of my cheek was bleeding and raw. It hurt bad. The room got wavy and the carpet started to suck me down into it. Sam was not there. We would have to go to California. Meredith and I would have to drive all the way across America to find Sam Malone. All the way to

Los Angeles. Meredith looked at me and tucked her hair behind her ears. She wore a little smirk and I knew then that she would do it. She would go with me, and we would go west.

"All right, well, thanks, I guess," I said to the bartender.

"Anytime, son."

I looked at him hard. "I am *not* your son," I said. Then I turned and walked out of the bar.

Outside, I sat down hard on the curb and held my head in my hands. I pressed my fingers into my eyelids until all I could see were dark red dots. After that, I looked up at the restaurant above the bar. It was all blurry and the red dots were still there, but I could see that it wasn't Melville's, the restaurant that John Allen Hill, Carla's sometimes-boyfriend, owns. It was a stupid looking restaurant called The Hampshire House. They had tricked me. They had made me believe that this was a real place, a place where I could go, and it would be exactly the same inside as it was on the show and Sam would be there and everyone would be there and everyone would know my name. But it wasn't that place. It wasn't it at all. It was just some dumb bar across from some dumb gardens with some dumb restaurant on top and no one was there and Sam especially wasn't there, because he was in Hollywood because he was a star.

"You're not going to cry, are you?" Meredith sat down beside me and lit a cigarette.

"No," I said, wiping my nose on my sleeve.

"That's good."

"They make it look so real on TV," I whispered.

"Yeah," she nodded, looking back at the bar. "They do."

"We have to go to Los Angeles," I said.

She blew a smoke ring that turned into a unicycle and pedaled away. "Do you have any idea how far that is?"

"Yes," I said. "It's the other ocean."

Meredith knocked the ash off her cigarette and we watched a horde of pigeons cluster around a woman in the park across the street. She was feeding them chunks of bread that she ripped from a loaf. More and more and more of them gathered around her, beating their wings together until it sounded like distant thunder. Then the woman gave up and just threw the whole loaf of bread at the mob of them. They pecked and clawed at each other, scrambling over one another to get at the bread in a crazy mess of feathers.

"Come on." Meredith tossed her cigarette into a storm drain. "Let's go get something to eat." She rubbed her belly. "This baby's hungry."

I got up and we started to walk. Gasoline rainbows swirled around on the road ahead of us. I didn't even look back at the *Cheers* bar.

# 14

Meredith and I ate at a diner called Lil Red's. There was a painting of a huge brown chicken on the window with a bright red comb. Not a comb like you brush your hair with, but the red wavy thing on top of chickens' heads is also called a comb. Turkeys have them too. I think it would be kind of neat to have a comb, especially if I could wave with it instead of my hands, but everyone would probably make fun of me and think I had some weird head disease, so maybe not. People always say, *Be careful what you wish for*. You don't always know what you really want when you're wishing for something you don't have. But I've thought about it a lot, and I know for sure that if I could only have one wish it would be to meet my real father. If I could have three wishes they would be:

1. Meet my real father

2. Have a dog

3. Have Gina and my father fall in love and get married and we would all live together and not move ever again

But nobody ever comes along and says, "Hey, kid, I'll grant you three wishes, what do you want?" At least not in real life, they don't. So I guess if you really want something, you have to go get it yourself. And that's why we were going to L.A.

Meredith got waffles with syrup and chocolate chips and a glass of whole milk and a coffee. I just got a chocolate milk because I wasn't hungry. It wasn't the good kind of chocolate milk, though, where it's all mixed together perfectly and there's no detectable powder or syrup. Someone at Lil Red's didn't know how to make chocolate milk properly, and the chocolate syrup dripped down the insides of the glass like dark blood. I watched Meredith eat, and she looked happy.

"What about *your* parents?" I said.

"What about them?" she said.

"Where are they? What do they do for work? Do you ever see them?"

"No," she said around a mouthful of waffle.

"How come?"

"They're dead."

"Oh. What happened?"

"My mom shot my dad and then killed herself when I was twelve."

"Holy moly."

She nodded, kept chewing.

"So you've been living at Bright Light since you were twelve?"

"Pretty much," she said.

"Wow."

"I was living with my brother and some of his friends for a while, but the social workers took me away because he was too young to be my legal guardian."

"And no one wanted to adopt you?"

"Are you kidding?" she snorted. "Nobody adopts older kids. They're damaged goods."

"Oh."

"*You're* even too old to get adopted now." She popped a chocolate chip into her mouth.

"That doesn't even matter because I don't need to get adopted. Gina's going to get out of the hospital soon and things will go back to normal. Probably by the time we get back from L.A. she'll be out, she'll probably already have a job by the time we get home."

"Are we seriously doing this, Tucker? Are we actually going to drive all the way to California?"

"Well, you'll be doing the driving, mostly."

She shook her head, took a sip of her coffee.

"What? You said you wanted a vacation! We can go to the beach. It'll be hot there. It's always sunny in Los Angeles. That's what they say."

"That's impossible," Meredith said. "It has to rain sometime."

"Does it, though?"

"Yes."

I saw a payphone in the corner and remembered my promise to Gina about calling every day. I dug a few quarters out of my sock. "I have to make a call," I said to Meredith and slid out of our booth.

"Hello?" By the way she answered, I could tell she'd been sleeping.

"Hi, Gina."

"Tucker! How are you, sunshine? Are you having a good time?"

"Yep. Pretty good."

"Oh that's good, sweetheart. And is Mary's family nice?"

The operator came on and told me I had one minute left for my call. I asked Gina if she was feeling better today and she said yes and told me about the lemon Jell-O she'd had for dessert.

"It had coconut flakes in it," she said.

"That sounds gross," I said.

"Oh, no. It was delicious. I'm going to make it for you sometime soon. You'll like it."

"But I hate coconut."

"You'll like this," she said.

"I'd better go, Gina."

"Oh, okay. You be good, okay, Tucker? Remember to say please and thank you and help out as much as you can with everything."

"Okay."

"I miss you," she said.

Then something clicked and the line went dead.

I walked back to our table.

"Ready to go?" Meredith said.

"Yep."

"You know this is crazy, right?"

"Yep."

"Like, a hundred-percent certifiably insane."

"Yep," I said, nodding.

"All right. As long as you know that."

I grinned at her and we walked out onto the street and got into the Caprice and drove out of Boston. The ocean shimmered behind us like a great, grey diamond as we made our way onto the turnpike.

\*\*\*

Near Albany, the Caprice's engine started to smoke. At first it was just a little bit of smoke wafting from the hood. Meredith and I both figured it would probably go away, and we'd check it at the next gas station, but it kept smoking and the smoke got darker, until pretty soon we couldn't see anything through the windshield but a big, black smoke cloud. Meredith pulled onto the shoulder and cut the engine.

"Shit," she said.

I stared out at the smoke.

"What should we do?" Meredith said.

"I don't know."

The car kept smoking.

"Do you think it's going to blow up?" she said.

I shrugged. "I guess it's possible."

"Fucking Chad. He's such a scum-fuck. He probably doesn't even put oil in this thing." She got out and slammed her door. Smoke billowed around her head. She tried to open the hood. "Ow! Jesus!" She put her fingers in her mouth. She looked over to the highway beside us and so did I. The cars were going by so fast they were blurry. The sky was inky-blue, almost black, and no one anywhere, except for Meredith, knew where I was.

Headlights flew by me like golden bullets. After a minute or two, Meredith got back in the car. Most of the smoke had cleared, but it still smelled like it was burning.

"I guess we'll just get to the next gas station and see what's wrong with it," she said.

"Okay." I nodded. "Good idea."

Meredith turned the key, and the engine chortled like it was laughing at us. She tried again, and it sniggered and gurgled. She tried again—same thing. The Caprice would not start. Meredith tried it about ten times and then beat her fist against the steering wheel and yelled mean things about Chad and Jesus and God and the car. Then she leaned her forehead against the steering wheel and closed her eyes. "I guess I deserve this," she said. The cars passing by outside sounded like they were saying, *shush, shush, shush.*

"Why would you deserve this?"

She turned her head to look at me, then turned forward again and closed her eyes. "I didn't borrow the car from Chad. I stole it."

"What?"

"I was going to put it back when we were done with it. It's more like borrowing, really."

"But Chad's your friend. What if he needed it for something important?"

"Chad's not my friend. He used to be my brother's best friend. Until he sold him out. It should be Chad in jail, not Steve."

"I think Chad's pretty nice."

"You don't know anything."

"I know he took me to the hospital when Gina got run over."

"That doesn't mean anything. The guy's a prick, all right? Trust me. I used to live with him. He's not a good person."

"He's trying," I said quietly.

Meredith shook her head.

"He's going to be mad."

"Ya *think?*"

"Will he know it was you who took it?"

"Probably," she said. "But he won't call the cops, at least. I know that for sure."

"What will he do when he finds out?"

"Kill me, probably," she said. "You too."

"But I didn't know—"

"Relax, I'm just fucking with you."

"Oh."

She sighed. "Nothing ever goes right for me, you know that? You should stay away from me. I'm bad luck. Here we are, stranded, totally fucked." Raindrops splattered against the windshield. Cars zinged by.

"It's going to be okay," I said. "Look at all these people with cars," I pointed to the highway. "Somebody must have room in their car for us."

Meredith put her hands over her stomach. Neither of us said anything for a few seconds. Then she said, "Get your stuff. Take everything. We'll never see this car again."

We took all of our things out, and at the last minute, I grabbed the baby-blue lace garter belt that was wrapped around the passenger sun-visor. I thought that it was probably special to Chad and maybe if I gave it to him when we got back to Niagara Falls, he wouldn't be so upset that Meredith had stolen his car and that we had abandoned it on the side of the road somewhere near Albany, New York.

\*\*\*

We stood on the shoulder with our thumbs out for about twenty minutes before Sherry picked us up. Sherry drove a red Pontiac Sunbird. Her hair was brown and fuzzy. She was going to Rochester to visit her aunt. There was a baby in the back of the Sunbird. It was the fattest baby I had ever seen. Its skin was all rolled up on itself. Its chins had chins. It looked like an alien that had swallowed three babies, that's how fat this baby was. I couldn't tell if it was a boy or a girl. Meredith sat up front, so I had to sit beside the baby. It mostly blew snot bubbles and gurgled and looked at me with googly eyes. There was nothing to be afraid of, because it was only a baby, but I didn't feel entirely comfortable sitting beside it. Meredith looked at it and said how cute it was, and Sherry seemed happy. I wondered if Meredith actually thought the baby was cute or if she was just saying that to be polite.

Sherry smacked her gum around in her mouth. She was a normal-looking lady—not skinny, but not fat, either. I couldn't see any extra chins on her. I looked at the baby. It looked like a miniature Jabba the Hutt. I hoped that when Meredith had her baby it looked nothing like this one.

Sherry told us about her job at the doll factory in Newark, New Jersey. She painted the lips and eyebrows on the dolls with a stencil and an airbrush machine and she stuck the glass eyes in and glued the eyelashes on and made sure all their faces and heads looked just right. She said she got to keep as many dolls as she wanted for her daughter, so I guess the baby was a girl.

Meredith said that it sounded like a cool job, but I knew Meredith would go crazy if she had to work in a doll factory, plus it was kind of creepy, so I knew she was definitely just being polite about that one. Being polite about stuff like that is not the same as lying, although it actually still is lying.

When Sherry asked us where we were headed, Meredith said

"Niagara Falls," and I said "Los Angeles" at the same time. Sherry laughed.

"We're going to California," I said.

"Jeez, that's a long way for a couple of kids like youse." She tilted the rear-view mirror to see me.

"I'm used to travelling," I said. "It's not that big a deal."

"You usually hitchhike?"

"Well, no," I said. "I usually take the bus."

"Because hitchhiking's a whole different story. Bad things can happen to people who hitchhike. Especially kids. I could've been a psychopath or a murderer picking you up. You just never know."

"Yeah, but you're not," I said.

"But I *could* be," she said.

"People are usually good," I said.

Sherry looked at Meredith. Meredith rolled her eyes, and they both shook their heads.

I looked at the baby then wished I hadn't. She started to cry. Her cries filled up the whole car.

"Hey, would you mind feeding Charity a little formula?" Sherry said. "Since you're back there. It'd save me having to stop."

"Um, sure. I guess," I said.

"Great! Just look in that bag beside you. There's a bottle in there. It's all mixed up already, maybe just give it a few shakes." She turned to Meredith. "Have to feed her formula now. She's allergic to breast milk *and* cow's milk. Best thing for her, doctor says. Did you know babies aren't supposed to have cow's milk?"

Meredith nodded. "I've heard that."

"Do you think you'll breast feed or do formula?"

"I ... I don't know," Meredith said.

"I think a combination of the two is the way to go, personally. Then, when you're not available, someone else can feed her." Sherry grinned.

I brought the bottle to the baby's mouth and she started sucking on it. Her eyes got wide and bright and then kind of glazed over. I had to tip it up a little bit for her to get it all out, but within a minute or two it was all gone and I put the empty bottle back in the bag.

"Thanks, hon. You're a doll," Sherry said.

"No problem." I leaned my head against the window and closed my eyes. When I opened them again we were stopped at a Texaco station and no one was in the car but the monster-baby and me.

I had been having a horrible dream. Sherry had crashed the car and she and Meredith were killed instantly. Their blood covered the windshield. I had to save the baby. I had to drag that fat-head baby out of a burning car and carry it to safety and it was so, so heavy. It weighed 80,000 pounds. It took all the strength I had to carry it. But I did. I saved it.

Meredith got back in the car then and a wave of relief washed over me.

"Sherry's in the bathroom," she said.

"Okay."

"Let's get out here and find another ride. She'll be turning off soon anyways."

The baby started to cry. Then it started to scream. It screamed and screamed and screamed and screamed. Its face turned red. Its body turned red. Then its face turned purple.

"Meredith?"

"What?"

"Do you really think that baby's cute?" I whispered.

She rolled her eyes. "Let's go." The quiet of the night outside the car was like stepping into a warm bath.

"Hey," Sherry said, jogging up to us. "Sorry I took so long. There was a line-up."

"I think we're going to look for another ride now," Meredith said. "But thanks so much, eh."

"Oh," Sherry said. She looked like someone had just punched her in the stomach. "Okay. If that's what you want."

"It is," Meredith said.

"Thanks," I said, and stuck out my hand. Sherry hesitated for a moment, then took it. Her handshake was like holding a dead fish. Sherry looked at Meredith and then pulled her in for a hug.

"Bye," Meredith said into Sherry's fuzz-head.

"Good luck to youse," Sherry said with a little catch in her voice. Then she pulled away and tooted the horn twice.

After we used the bathrooms and bought some snacks, Meredith and I stood in front of the store under the red and blue neon sign that buzzed and flashed on and off and spelled out O-P-E-N one letter at a time.

# 15

"Are you sure you want to go to L.A.?" Meredith said.

"Positive."

"I mean, *really* sure?"

"I'm a hundred-percent sure."

"It's okay if you want to change your mind. No one will blame you. We can probably even make it back to the falls tonight."

"Meredith, listen, I've never been more sure of anything in my whole entire life. I'm going to L.A. to find out if Sam Malone is my father. You don't have to come. I mean, I hope you do, I want you to, but I understand if you don't want to."

"Don't you mean the actor, Ted Danson?"

"No. I mean Sam Malone."

Meredith lit a cigarette and took a long drag and blew it out the side of her mouth while she stared at me, her green eyes all narrowed and suspicious. "You're serious."

"Yes."

"How the hell do you think you're going to find *him?*"

"Go to Paramount Pictures in Hollywood, just like the bartender said."

"And what if once you get there, nothing's like you thought it would be?"

"Well, this is the most important thing I've ever done. And I have to do it. Plus, Gina could die. And I don't want to have to live at Bright Light until I'm nineteen."

"Can't blame you for that," she said. Meredith sighed then looked at me with a lopsided smile. "You know what I like about you?"

"No," I said.

"You're kind of crazy."

I shrugged.

"But in a good way."

We waited in front of the gas station store for a good long while. I'm not sure how long. Long enough for Meredith to smoke three cigarettes and for both of us to finish our snacks and drinks. Some people pulled in for gas and left and some people came in to buy cigarettes and coffee, but most of them were in a hurry and none of them were quite right. Then along came a guy in a blue Toyota 4Runner. He wore a John Deere hat, jeans, and flip-flops, and whistled the song from *The Little Mermaid* as he filled his tank. He smiled and nodded as he passed us and went into the store to pay for his gas.

"I think we should ask him," Meredith said.

"I don't know. What if he's a creep? And besides, who wears flip-flops in April?"

"He's not a creep."

"How can you know that?"

"I get these feelings about people," she said. "I can't explain it. I can just tell. He'll be good."

Lyle was from Maine, and he was going to his friend Ricky's wedding in Cincinnati, Ohio, but he had to drive all night because he'd left Maine late because there was a six-foot swell and Lyle was a surfer and he'd wanted to stay for it. But he had to be in Cincinnati for the wedding at eleven a.m. because he was the best man. The best thing about Lyle was that he had a big old Golden Retriever named Belinda in the back of the 4Runner. She was friendly as anything, and there were a bunch of blankets and pillows back there too, so I climbed into the back and let Meredith sit up front with Lyle, which she probably preferred because he smiled a lot and had dimples in his cheeks, and I don't know anything about teenage girls except that they go bananas for guys with dimples. I lay down and Belinda licked my hand, then I scratched her behind the ears and she wagged her tail so much that it slapped against my leg and whacked against the inside of the truck, but eventually she calmed down and turned in a circle three times then lay down beside me and we fell asleep like that.

When I woke up, I peeked around at Meredith to make sure she was okay and that Lyle hadn't done anything creepy to her. She was conked out with her mouth hanging open and looked peaceful enough. Her hair splayed out around her shoulders in all directions. Her hands were folded over her belly. She had her big black hoodie on so you couldn't really see too much of her belly, but you could see something, like she was hiding a small pumpkin there. I wondered if most people could tell that Meredith was pregnant or if they just thought she was a bit fat.

"How're you doing back there, champ? You need to stop or anything?"

"I'm okay," I said.

"Okey dokey," Lyle said. "You just let me know if you need anything."

And then I felt guilty for thinking bad things about Lyle because he really was an all right guy. Belinda stirred in her sleep and kicked her legs and I wondered what she was dreaming about. I petted her big face and head and watched as her black lips curled up into a smile.

"Lyle?"

"Yeah?" Lyle looked at me in the rear-view mirror.

"Do you have a dad?"

"I did." He nodded. "He passed away last year."

"How did he die?"

Lyle cleared his throat. "Car accident," he said. "Drinking and driving."

"Oh," I said.

"He killed a little kid too. A three-year-old boy." Lyle squinted into the oncoming headlights.

"Did you get to talk to him before he died?" I asked.

"Yeah, I did, actually."

"What did you say?"

"I told him he was an idiot and that I loved him."

"Did you forgive him?" I said.

"I don't know," Lyle said. "I think I'm still trying to."

Then we were both quiet for a while and the sky started to lighten around the edges. Lyle turned on the radio and it was "Stand by Me" by Ben E. King, which is an old song but still really good, and Lyle didn't change the station and I was glad for it.

The sky was lemon yellow as we pulled into the Motel 6 parking lot in Cincinnati. Belinda stretched and yawned and shoved her face into my hand. Lyle got out and then Meredith and Belinda and I did too. He put his arms over his head and stretched back, looking up to the sky behind him. He patted his thigh and Belinda ran to him and nosed his leg.

"Well, guys, it's been a slice," Lyle said, grinning and slapping Belinda's butt. She whined and did a little dog-dance around us.

"Thanks so much for the ride," Meredith said.

"Yeah, thanks, Lyle," I said.

"Hey, no sweat. You can probably grab breakfast somewhere around here." He looked up and down the strip. "Then just stand on that side of the road, this road we came in on, and you'll probably be in Tennessee before Ricky can say I do." Lyle laughed and so did we.

I said goodbye to Belinda and gave her a good scratch behind the ears and let her lick my face. Meredith gave her a couple of pats on the head, and then Lyle whistled and Belinda ran to him and he gave us a little wave then turned toward the office of the motel and we went the other way down the street.

We found a place that was open called The Diner on Sycamore

and slid into a red booth next to the window. There was a jukebox in the corner playing "Hit the Road Jack," and I'm pretty sure it was Ray Charles singing it. I like Ray Charles a lot because he's proof that just because you're blind doesn't mean you can't play piano and also be a great singer, which pretty much means that anyone can do anything if they really, really want to.

"Wasn't he great?" Meredith said. "I told you he would be good."

"Yep. You were right."

"And wasn't he beautiful?"

"I don't know," I said.

"*Come on!*"

"I don't really know what makes a person beautiful or not," I said.

"Seriously?"

I shrugged.

"I wish we could've rode with him the whole way," she said.

"I liked his dog."

Meredith rolled her eyes. Then the waitress came and took our order. She wore a nametag that read "Andie." One of her eyes was brown and the other one was blue, and I thought that probably qualified her as beautiful. Andie had curly blonde hair piled up on top of her head in a loose bun. After she wrote down our order, she stuck her pencil into her bun and walked away. I watched to see if the pencil would fall out, but it didn't, it stayed put. I thought maybe when my hair got a bit longer, I would try putting it up like that and sticking pencils and pens and markers and glue sticks and whatever else I wanted in there, and if it stayed, then I wouldn't even have to get a new pencil case for school. I could just stick everything in my hair, and it would never get lost.

"Do you think we should call Chad?" I said.

"Why would we call Chad?"

"I don't know, to tell him about his car. In case he wants to go get it or something."

"Fuck Chad," Meredith said. Then our food arrived, and we didn't say anything more about it.

After we finished eating, Meredith ordered us two chocolate shakes to go because she said we didn't know how long we would have to wait for our next ride, and we didn't want to be stranded on the side of the highway with nothing to eat or drink. I knew that Meredith would be a good mom because she thought about stuff like that.

The sun was shining and the spring air had that warm-dirt smell in it, and we didn't have to wait very long for our next ride. I wasn't even finished my milkshake before a guy in a white Dodge van stopped in front of us. He popped open the passenger door and gave us a big smile and said, "Hop in, kids!"

Meredith and I looked at each other.

"What do you think?" I said to her out of the side of my mouth.

"I don't know," she said.

"Where ya headed?"

"Los Angeles," I said.

"Well, I'm going to Oklahoma City if you want to come," the driver said.

Meredith whispered, "That's a long way from here. We should go."

So we got in the van. This time, I sat up front.

"Oh, *shit*," Meredith said as she climbed into the back.

I turned around to see what she was worried about, and there must have been 200 guns back there. Shotguns, handguns, rifles, a whole crap-load of guns.

"Don't worry," the guy said. "They're not loaded."

"Are you sure?" Meredith said.

"Not a single one of those is loaded, swear on my life. They're for the shows."

"What shows?" Meredith said, still standing up in the back of the van.

"The gun shows. I drive around and take these babies to different gun shows in every state. Collectors look at them, sometimes buy them, we talk about the NRA, the second amendment, all that good stuff."

"What's the second amendment?" I said.

"You're kidding, right?" he said.

I shook my head.

"Jesus, Mary, and Joseph, what are they teaching you kids in school these days? You don't know your own *constitution?* The Bill of Rights?"

Meredith sat down and slid the back door closed, hard. "We're Canadian," she said.

"Oh. Well, that explains it." He started driving. He had a buzz cut and kind of a goofy-looking face. He wore a grey T-shirt that said ARMY across the front. He told us his name was Timothy and he'd been a soldier in the Gulf War. He'd been awarded a Bronze Star for valor and a bunch of other medals I can't remember. "Ate, slept, and shit in the desert for four months," he said. "After that, you can do just about anything." He hated Iraq and what he had to do there, which was kill people. Kids too. He hated the United States government and everything they stood for. He said the US government was the worst bunch of scum-sucking hypocrites in the entire world.

"So how come you're going to Oklahoma City?" Meredith asked.

"I could tell you," he said. "But then I'd have to kill you."

I'm not sure if he was joking or not.

We drove for a long time, and Timothy talked a lot, mostly about guns and the government and Kuwait. Meredith fell asleep, and I half-listened to Timothy while I watched the farms and fields and rivers pass by the window.

Sometime in the late afternoon, Meredith said she needed a washroom and I remembered that I had to call Gina. Timothy said no problem and stopped at the next gas station. I found a payphone in the back of the store and called the hospital. I let it ring about a thousand times until *finally* someone picked up, but it wasn't Gina, it was Heather. We talked for a bit and she asked me if I wanted her to wake Gina up and I said no but to tell her I called. She told me she would, and then we hung up.

We got back in the van and had driven about ten minutes when Timothy looked back at Meredith and then turned to me and said, "Either of you guys ever shoot a gun?"

"No," Meredith said.

I shook my head.

"You want to?" Timothy asked.

"No," Meredith said. "Definitely not."

I shrugged.

"How old are you?" he said.

"Eleven," I said.

"And no one's taught you how to shoot a gun yet? What do you guys do up in Canada anyways?"

"I thought you said these weren't loaded," Meredith said.

"Well, they're not, but I have ammo with me," he said. "Never leave home without it." He grinned. "That's my constitutional right."

"God bless America," Meredith said. And I could tell without even looking at her that she was rolling her eyes back there.

Timothy pulled over. He opened the back doors and started banging and clanking things around.

"I don't like this," Meredith said.

"What should we do?" I said.

"I don't know," she said. "Get out and run?"

"What if he shoots us? He got all those medals in the war. He's probably a sharp shooter."

"Why would he shoot us? We haven't done anything to him."

"I don't know, just because we're running away he might shoot us."

Then Timothy yelled, "This is going to be so fun! You guys are going to love this."

Meredith looked at me, her green eyes wide and bright with fear.

"Okay," I whispered. "The most important thing is not to panic."

"Come on, get out of there!" Timothy came around and slid Meredith's side door open.

"Hi," Meredith said.

"Come on, we're going to have some fun," he said. "I'm going to teach you kids how to shoot." He held a plastic bag full of soup cans and a blue duffel bag. He extended one hand to Meredith. She hesitated, then took it and stepped out of the van. Then I got out too, and we followed Timothy over the ditch and down a little trail into the woods.

Meredith and I shot each other looks of doubt and terror every few yards. My knees were shaking so much I was afraid I'd fall down. But I knew that running would be a bad idea, and I didn't know what else to do. *Don't panic. Don't panic. Don't panic,* I told myself.

"She's pregnant," I said, pointing at Meredith.

"Oh," Timothy stopped and turned around. He eyed Meredith up and down. "Congratulations," he said.

"Thanks," she muttered.

Timothy nodded and turned around and kept marching us through the woods. I could hear little birds and squirrels skittering under the brush, and I wondered if they would be among the last sounds I ever heard. Finally, we came to a clearing. Timothy put the duffel bag down and told us to wait, then ran to set up the soup cans on an old stone fence about fifty feet away.

"Do you have any *feelings* about him?" I said to Meredith.

She glared at me. "I'm scared too," she said. "But I think it'll be okay."

"You *think?* What if it's not?"

"Then it's too late anyways," she said.

Timothy ran back to us, grinning. "Ready?" he said as he unzipped the duffel and took out a handgun. It was black and humongous and, I realized, loaded.

"I don't know," Meredith said. "Isn't this kind of dangerous?"

"The only thing more dangerous than having a gun is not having a gun," he said. "Now this here is a Beretta M9 semi-automatic. This is the official pistol of the United States Army. You know why?"

I shook my head.

"Because it's tough as tits, that's why," he said. "This little beast can survive temperatures from minus forty to a hundred and forty. You can bash it with a brick, drop it in the ocean, bury it in the sand—or snow, if you're in Canada." He laughed. "Don't hurt it one bit. Takes a lickin' and keeps on tickin'."

I nodded.

"Want to hold it?"

I shook my head.

"Come on!" he said. "Won't hurt you. Safety's on." He held it out to me.

I hesitated.

"Come *on.*"

I took it. It was heavy and huge in my hands. My hands were sweaty, and my heart boinged around in my chest like a super-bounce. I looked up at Timothy, and he was smiling down at me. I held the gun out for him to take back.

"I'll take the first shot," he said. "Watch what I do."

"Okay," I said.

"First, I take the safety off. This is the safety. See, on, off." He flicked a little black switch up and down.

"Okay."

"Then, with the safety off, you can cock the hammer back. This is the hammer."

"Hammer. Got it," I said.

"Now, I'm going to hold it with two hands. Are you right or left handed?"

"Right," I said.

"That's fine," Timothy said. "Okay. That's all there is to it. Now I'm ready to shoot. Oh, cover your ears."

Meredith and I pressed our hands against our ears.

Timothy closed one eye and shot the gun. It was the loudest sound I'd ever heard. It was like a building had just blown up beside me. Then it happened again. And again. And again. And again. Little gold shells flipped out of the gun like coins and landed at my feet. He took five shots, and five soup cans flew off the fence like tin birds. He switched the safety back on and turned to me. I think he asked who wanted to go next, but I couldn't hear anything except a high-pitched ringing in my ears. The world was a fire-alarm drill.

I looked over at Meredith and saw her shake her head no. My hearing came back slowly.

"I hate guns. I can't do it," Meredith said.

"Why would you hate guns?" Timothy asked.

"Because guns kill people," she said.

"That's what they're designed to do, Meredith," he said. "You can't hate something for doing what it's made to do."

"I can if I want to," she said. "It's my constitutional right." She turned away, looked up at the sky. We followed her gaze to a hawk soaring above us. Timothy turned back to Meredith and looked at her hard.

"I'll try it," I said. I was shocked to hear the words come out of my mouth because I hadn't planned on saying them.

Timothy grinned at me. "That's the spirit." He slapped me on the shoulder then handed me the gun.

Electric neon blood coursed through my veins as I held it.

"Now, the safety's on. And the hammer's not cocked, but as you know, it *is* loaded," Timothy said. "There are many steps you need to take before you can take a shot."

"Okay," I said. Every cell in my body vibrated.

"So, first you want to get into a good position, a solid shooting stance."

I adjusted my feet and shoulders and held onto the gun as if it were a live thing that could jump out of my hands at any moment.

"That's it, that's it." He adjusted my grip on the gun a little. "Now, what do you want to do?"

"Take off the safety," I said.

"That's right. So, take off the safety."

I flipped the switch up. The gun seemed to grow hot in my hands. I realized my unlimited power. I could do anything. Get anything. Take anything. Say anything I wanted to anybody. I was holding a loaded gun, and the world was my cheeseburger.

"Now what?" Timothy said.

"Cock the hammer," I said.

"That's right. So pull it back."

I pulled it back.

"Good, now take your time. Aim carefully. Take deep breaths and focus, then depress the trigger as you exhale."

I had to pull the trigger hard, but when I did the gun exploded in my hand like a bomb. I don't know what happened. It was like another

Tucker crawled inside me. I shot five times in a row, and then I was screaming and yelling with the thrill of it all. I handed the gun back to Timothy and ran around in circles waving my arms in the air. I had actually hit one of the cans! I couldn't believe it. It was a great feeling, to have shot a gun. I was glad I had done it.

"Woohoo!" I yelled and did a little dance and ran up to Meredith and hugged her.

She pushed me away. "All right, can we get out of here now?" she said.

Timothy was laughing. As we walked back to the van, I felt like I was walking on stilts. I was twelve feet tall. I was strong and big and so, so, alive.

# 16

The next time Timothy stopped for gas, Meredith piped up from the back of the van, "We'll wait here." Then she pinched me on the elbow.

"Okay," Timothy said. "You want anything?"

"No thanks, we're good," Meredith said.

"Alrighty then. Be right back."

Meredith slid the door open as she watched Timothy go into the store. "Let's get out of here, that guy's a fucking psycho," she said.

"Timothy?" I said.

"Yeah, *Timothy.*"

"He's all right," I said. "He just really likes guns. He's harmless."

As soon as Timothy had gone around the side of the store to the bathrooms, Meredith said, "Suit yourself, I'm out of here." She grabbed her stuff and ran. I had no choice but to follow her.

We crouched in a cluster of bushes behind the store, clutching our backpacks to our chests. Cigarette butts and pop cans littered the ground.

"Now what?" I said.

"We'll just wait here until he goes away and then find another ride."

"But he was going all the way to Oklahoma."

"Who cares? He was insane. He let an eleven-year-old shoot a gun! He could've killed us, Tucker! He probably *would* have if we'd stuck around any longer."

"I thought he was okay," I shrugged. Maybe she was right, maybe she wasn't. There was no way of ever knowing.

We waited in the bushes for what seemed like a year. Meredith went out first to peek around the corner to check if his van was still there.

"It's gone," she said, waving me out.

We went into the store and got chips and sandwiches and ate our dinner on yellow milk crates behind the store. The light from the sky was beginning to fade as Meredith lit a cigarette. "I can't believe you shot a gun," she said.

"Not just any gun. A Beretta M9," I said. "The official pistol of the United States Armed Forces."

"Tough as tits," she said, impersonating Timothy. Then we both cracked up. "Come on," Meredith said as she stood up. "Let's go find a ride."

"Let me know if you get any *feelings* about this next one," I said.

"Shut up," Meredith said.

We leaned against the brick wall at the side of the store. The clouds were low and murky. I didn't know which city we were in, but not a lot of people were coming into the gas station.

"We'd better find someone before it gets dark," Meredith said.

Then an old black guy in a gold Buick Regal pulled up.

"How about him?" I said.

"Let's just watch him for a minute first," Meredith said.

He was probably a hundred years old. His movements were slow and careful as he got out of his car. He looked around, and I could tell, even from that far away, that his eyes were filled with a certain sadness.

"Okay," Meredith said. "Let's ask him." We walked up to him, but not too fast. It was as though we were both afraid to startle him. Meredith cleared her throat, and he looked at her. "Um, excuse me, sir. We were wondering if you're going west?"

He nodded.

"Would you happen to have room in your car for us?"

The man looked inside his car and then back at Meredith and me. He nodded again.

"Oh, that's great," she said. "Thank you so much."

I smiled at him and he nodded. Then he put the nozzle back and went into the store to pay for his gas.

Meredith got in the front, and I got in the back. The car smelled like humbug candies and lemons. The interior was soft caramel leather. I sat behind the man and could see little tufts of grey hair poking out under his cap.

"So where are you headed?" Meredith asked as he pulled onto the freeway.

He glanced down at the map that sat on the armrest between them and pointed to a dot. Meredith leaned closer to inspect it. "Dodge City, Kansas?"

He nodded.

"All right, we'll take it."

The back of the Buick was as big as my bunk bed at Bright Light. I was suddenly so tired, all I could think about was stretching out across the seat and going to sleep. There was hardly any light left in the sky. Meredith yawned, then I yawned, then the man yawned. I don't know why yawning is contagious, but it is. It's easier to make someone yawn than to make someone laugh.

"Would it be all right if I lay down back here?" I asked the man.

He nodded with his eyes.

"Thanks," I said.

The man didn't play the radio or a cassette, and it was quiet and peaceful in the car. I watched the first few stars appear out the window. The evening star, which is not a star at all, but the planet Venus, was the last thing I saw before I conked out.

\*\*\*

When I woke up, Meredith was sleeping stretched out on the opposite end of the backseat with her feet resting beside my face. Her socks had little purple daisies on them, and there was a hole in the heel of the left one. Her feet smelled like corn chips. I could see the rise and fall of her pumpkin-belly with each breath. We were parked in front of an old ramshackle house whose siding was falling off. There was a gigantic willow tree beside the car, and the light of the moon shone through the branches like fingers reaching down to poke us.

I got out and peed behind the Buick. Then I took a little look around. There was a mountain of old window frames piled up in the yard, but all the glass in them was missing. Beside that, there was a claw-foot bathtub with geraniums growing out of it. One of the feet on the tub was wearing a yellow rubber boot. An old wooden swing dangled from the willow tree, and I sat on it while I looked at the moon, which looked like a broken dinner plate. A breeze rustled the willow branches and wispy clouds floated in front of the moon and I got the strange feeling that I was inside somebody else's dream.

I thought about Gina and hoped that she was okay. I hoped she would be a hundred-percent well again by the time I got back from Los Angeles. She would be mad as hell at me, but she would get over it, eventually. Maybe the two of us would even go visit Sam Malone together sometime. Maybe she would decide that it was finally time to forgive him for whatever it was he'd done.

I sat in the swing until I got tired again, then I got back in the car and tried to lie down without bumping Meredith too much. She groaned, but she didn't wake up. I heard an owl hoot nearby and figured that he must be watching over us.

\*\*\*

When I woke up, I thought the sky was on fire. But it was only

the sunrise. It was the most beautiful one I had ever seen. I woke Meredith up to see it.

"Wow," she said, rubbing her eyes. "Where are we?"

"I don't know," I said. "There's a house here."

"But we weren't invited in, right?"

I shrugged.

"We should go," she said.

"Okay."

Meredith wrote a note that said *THANK YOU!* to our driver on the back of a gas receipt we found in the cup-holder. She drew a little heart where the dot in the exclamation point should've been and left it on his seat. We got our stuff out of the car and started to walk west. We walked for a long time, and no cars passed us. Meredith scrunched up her face and put her hands under her belly like she was carrying a bowling ball. We heard a rooster crowing and some birds chattering, but other than that, it was pretty quiet. When we got into the town, it was like we had stepped back in time. All of the buildings were old saloon-style like the kind you see in western movies.

"What *is* this place?" Meredith said.

"I don't know, but I think I like it."

"Me too," she said.

"I feel like I should be riding a horse."

"Definitely. You should be. Where can we find some horses around here?" she looked around, shielding her eyes from the sun. "I want a Palomino."

"Any pal of yours is a Palomino," I said.

Meredith laughed and punched me in the shoulder, but not hard.

I stopped to peer in the window as we passed The Gunfighters Wax Museum.

"This place is almost as weird as Niagara Falls," Meredith said.

Before long, we came to a sign that pointed one way to the I-70 and the opposite way to town. "What should we do?" I said.

"Well, Tucker, I think we should get the heck out of Dodge."

I laughed and so did she as we walked along the road out of town under the wide, red sky.

# 11

We had to walk for about two hours before a car stopped for us. It was a blue Toyota Tercel. The lady inside was middle-aged, maybe twenty-nine, thirty. She had messy black hair and a jean jacket that had things written on it in black permanent marker.

"Want a ride?" she called out her window.

"Yeah!" I said. I got in the front and Meredith got in the back. There was a laundry basket heaped high with clothes in the backseat. The car smelled like a million cigarettes had been smoked in it.

"I'm Stacey," she said and shook my hand. "That there's Camden."

I looked back and was surprised to see a little kid sitting in the basket under the pile of laundry. He was probably three or four. He was scrawny and his hair was the colour of sand.

"Where're y'all headed?" Stacey asked as she began to drive.

"Hollywood," I said.

"Wow, gonna be movie stars, are ya? We like movies, don't we, Camden?"

"Yup," he said, nodding hard.

"We're going to find my father, actually," I said.

"Oh wow. That's cool," she said.

"Where are you going?" Meredith asked.

"Oh, we're just going over to my mama's. She lives in Garden City. It's about an hour from here."

"Grandma has a TV," Camden said.

"That's right," said Stacey. "My ex took everything when he left us. Washer-dryer, television, VCR, stereo, took the frigging dishes and cutlery, too. Imagine leaving your own kid without any plates to eat off of."

"Sounds like a loser," Meredith said.

"Oh, he is! He's a big fat loser."

"Daddy's not fat," Camden said.

"He will be one day, sweetie," said Stacey as she changed lanes. "Sorry, I just have to stop for gas here."

"No problem," Meredith said.

Stacey pulled into a Mobil and got out to pump the gas. I watched her in my side mirror as she leaned down next to the nozzle and took deep breaths, inhaling the wavy fumes.

"Meredith," I said through my teeth.

Meredith turned to look out her window at Stacey. "Oh, Jesus," she said.

"Jesus loves me!" Camden said. "Know how I know?"

"No," Meredith said.

"Because the *bible* tells me so!"

Meredith nodded and said, "That's good."

Then Stacey took an empty Gatorade bottle out of her purse. She put a little bit of gas in it, then put the nozzle back on the hook and had a big whiff out of the bottle. She saw that Meredith and I were watching her, and a dark blush spread over her face. She screwed on the lid of the bottle and shoved it in her purse, then ran into the store to pay. When she got back in the car, she threw us each a glass bottle of Coke, Camden too. She looked sheepish. "I'm sorry about that," she said. "It's just, since Ted left and everything, I've been a real mess." Stacey's eyes were the colour of peacock's necks. "It's stupid, I know. It just ... it helps. You know?"

Meredith nodded and helped Camden open his bottle of Coke.

When we got to Stacey's mom's house, her mom's boyfriend, Hal, was about to leave. He said he'd give us a ride to the highway. Hal drove a green Ford Ranger. He had longish white hair and a white moustache. He was skinny but looked strong. I wondered if my hair would ever turn white like Hal's and I decided that it would be okay if it did.

As we were rolling out of Garden City, a little sparrow flew smack into the windshield and startled us all. Hal shook his head and turned on the wipers, smearing blood across the glass. Meredith put one hand over her belly and closed her eyes. No one said much for the rest of the drive. We listened to the country station. All of the songs were sad. Gina says she doesn't like country for that reason. Most of the songs are so, so sad. But I like it okay, when I'm in the right mood.

Hal let us out where the 81 intersects with the 54. "You'll be all right here," he said. "Town's just a quarter mile that way if you need anything."

"Okay, thanks for the ride," I said.

Meredith waved.

"Adios," Hal said and drove away.

We stood at the side of the road. Meredith smoked a cigarette. I kicked rocks. No cars passed. There was nothing to see for thousands of miles but fields and sky and a never-ending strip of cracked pavement. Watching white wisps of cirrus clouds move across the Kansas sky makes your heart ache. I don't know why.

Meredith took a hairbrush out of her backpack and started to brush her hair right there on the side of the road. Then she took out a little mirror and her eye makeup and put that on. I watched her pull down her bottom eyelid and it sicked me out. I don't know how girls can jab a pencil practically right into their eyeball to put makeup on. I could never be a girl.

After what seemed like a hundred hours, a little black Geo Metro came by. The driver was around twenty and had spiky black hair. When Meredith leaned in the window to talk to him, I could see that *he* was wearing makeup. Even his nails were painted black. *And* he was wearing black lipstick. His nose was pierced, but not like Meredith's, it was pierced *between* the two nostrils, like a bull. Meredith talked to him for a minute then stepped back from the car to talk to me. "Do you want to go with him?"

"Not really," I whispered. "He looks weird."

"It's just a fashion," Meredith said, lowering her voice. "It's called goth."

"It's weird," I said.

"Sometimes weird looking people are the most normal, and the normal looking people are the weirdest," Meredith said.

"Then how are you supposed to know who actually *is* weird?"

She shrugged. "You just have to trust your feelings, I guess."

"I don't have any feelings," I said.

"You have feelings, Tucker."

"Yeah, but not about people."

"Sure you do."

"I don't know if I do," I shrugged.

"Well, this is the first car we've seen in over an hour so I think we should go with him."

"Okay," I said. "But if he chops us up in little pieces, I'm blaming you."

Meredith rolled her eyes and opened the passenger door, and I got in the back.

"I'm Chris," he said, shaking our hands. Meredith smiled at him and I wondered if she had a big crush on him already like she'd had on Lyle. Maybe goth was something beautiful. It was hard to tell. Chris wore a necklace that looked like a dog collar. It was black with big silver spikes. If you leaned in to hug him, you'd get a spike jammed in your throat. So I guess he didn't want anybody to hug him. Or maybe he wished he was a dog instead of a man, which probably a lot of people do. He ate gummy worms out of a plastic bag that he held between his legs. He offered Meredith and me some, and we both took a handful. We didn't say too much for the rest of the trip because I guess part of being goth is that you don't talk a lot.

He let us out near Santa Rosa, and another woman picked us up right away. She drove a blue Toyota Corolla and had two boys around my age. I sat in the back with the boys, and Meredith sat shotgun. The boys' names were Dylan and Eric and they were both glued to their Game Boys. I tried to talk to them but they both just scowled at me and went back to their games. They were from a town in Colorado with a name that sounds like a piece of farm machinery but is actually a type of flower. The lady talked non-stop to Meredith about her son and his friend and how they were such troublemakers, but really good kids deep down and how she wasn't looking forward to them becoming teenagers in a few years but how she knew that in the end, it would all be worth it. After a while she turned around and said, "Dylan, why don't you let Tucker try your Game Boy. You've been playing for long enough now."

"No way," Dylan said. "I'm just about to beat level eight."

"Dylan? Remember? We talked about this."

"It's okay," I said. "I'm not very good at video games anyways."

"*See*," Dylan said. "He'll just die." He elbowed me in the ribs then went back to his game, and he and Eric didn't look up for the rest of the ride. I secretly wished that I *could* play Game Boy, but it was two against one back there, and I didn't want them to gang up on me.

The lady let us out at a shopping plaza in Albuquerque, and the air outside the car smelled fresh and clean. I felt kind of dizzy and sick, probably because there was no fresh air in that car and I'd been breathing everybody else's carbon dioxide for too long.

# 18

"What a bunch of dweebs," Meredith said as the lady drove off, tapping the horn. "And the *mom*. *God*. I thought I was going to have to throw myself out of the car. She wouldn't shut up about how great those kids are."

"I know."

"And let me tell you, those kids are not great. Those kids are going to be brain dead in a couple of years if they're not already."

I laughed.

"I'm never letting my kid play video games," she said. "They turn people into zombies."

"What about TV?"

"TV's okay," Meredith said.

I felt strangely relieved, knowing that Meredith's kid would be allowed to watch TV.

"Not the news though," she said. "That shit's fucked up."

We walked across the parking lot. The lights of Albuquerque glittered all around us. We came to a McDonald's and went inside. We both got personal pizzas and milk and sat at a booth and ate our pizzas, and they were good and hot. It was late, I'm not sure how late. Not many people came in. A lady and a man came in together, and they both had black eyes. I wondered if they gave them to each other. Most of the people who came in were drunk. I could tell because they couldn't say their words properly and had to hold onto the counter to stand up. I'm not really sure why adults get drunk because it makes them all so stupid. But maybe that's another one of those things that I'll understand when I get older. It takes a lot of years to learn all the things in the world. I watched Meredith as she finished her dinner.

"What's the worst thing that's ever happened to you?" I said.

She looked up at me with her straw still in her mouth. "Why would you ask me that?"

"Just tell me," I said.

She set down her drink. "My parents, I guess."

"Yeah, that's pretty bad."

"What about you?"

I shrugged.

"Come on."

"Not having a dad, I guess. Except that didn't really *happen* to me. More like, it *didn't* happen."

"Yeah, that sucks. But, hey, if it makes you feel any better, I don't have a dad either," she said.

"But you *did* have one."

"Yes, I did."

"And that's better than never having one at all."

"Depends," she said.

"On what?"

"On how nice they are."

"Was your dad nice?"

"He was sometimes nice and sometimes really mean and we just never knew what we were going to get."

"I'm sorry about what happened to your parents," I said.

"Thanks," she said. "Come on, let's get out of here."

We finished the last bites of our pizzas, and I threw out our stuff and put the trays on top of the garbage bin like you're supposed to. Then we walked toward the lights of the city.

Eventually we came upon a little place called the Motel Blue. It was blue, like you would expect, but it was pure, pure blue, like the best sky on the best day of the best summer ever. They had it all lit up with spotlights so it glowed electric blue out into the night. It cost forty dollars, and we got a room with two beds. I let Meredith have the first shower. While she was in the bathroom, I checked the drawer of the nightstand for a bible because Gina says that's how you know you're staying in a reputable motel. Although I'm not exactly sure *why* Gina thinks that since we're not religious, and I haven't even been baptized, which means that I'm going straight to hell when I die, if there is a hell. A girl named Jessica Timbermore in Medicine Hat told me that, and then she and a bunch of other kids made fun of me for not being baptized and called me a heathen. When I told Gina about it, I asked her what to do, and she told me to tell them to get stuffed, so I did and after that none of them would pick me for their team or partner up with me for partner activities or anything, but I didn't really care because we moved away not too long afterwards.

When I opened the drawer, the bible was there, and I was relieved to see it. It was blue, like everything else in the room. I picked it up and wondered, not for the first time, who the Gideons were and how they got into every single motel room in the world. I figured they were probably like little elves who snuck around slipping bibles into drawers of rooms that people had left unlocked. I wondered how many Gideons there were and decided that if I ever met one, I would ask him about the bibles. Then Meredith came out of the bathroom, yelling, wearing only a towel.

"Help me, Tucker!" she had another towel attached to her face. "It's caught on my nose ring! It's pulling it out! I can't get it off!"

"Okay, okay." I stood up and went to her.

"It's ripping out!"

"Let me see." There was blood around the nose ring. But it wasn't ripped completely out.

"Can you get it?"

I moved the towel-threads a tiny bit off the ring.

"OW!"

I pulled my hand back.

"GET IT OFF!"

I tried again, and this time I got it. Meredith covered her nose with her hands and ran back into the bathroom, slamming the door behind her.

"Is it bleeding a lot?" I yelled.

She didn't answer. I heard water running and her swearing.

She came out after a while with her clothes on and her nose was red, but she had cleaned off the blood and the ring was still in.

"Let me see," I said, and examined it up close. "I think it'll heal just fine."

"How can you tell?"

I shrugged. "That's what bodies are made to do."

She sighed. "Thanks for helping me get it off."

"That's what friends are for," I said.

Then I showered and brushed my teeth and it felt good to be clean and smell like the honey-vanilla motel shampoo. We tried to watch TV for a while but the only things on were televangelists and infomercials for ab-machines, and you can only watch those for so long. I turned off the TV and tried reading the Gideon bible for a bit, Meredith put her Walkman on, and eventually, we both fell asleep.

When I woke up, it felt like I had rocks in my stomach and something was terribly wrong but I didn't know what. Then I looked out the window and saw the bright sky. I knew that it was morning, and then I realized that I had broken my promise to Gina—I hadn't called her the day before. I watched the cars rush by and tried to think of what to say to her. Tried to make up a story that would make sense about why I hadn't called and why I wasn't coming back to Niagara Falls today or the next day or the day after that. The sun glinted off the windshields of cars and pierced my brain. I looked over at Meredith. She was sleeping so hard you'd think she was dead. She was sleeping for two now.

I opened my backpack and took out my shoebox and got Charlie out of it. I lay down again and put him next to me on the pillow and petted him. He looked at me with his puppy dog eyes. But he didn't judge me. That was the best thing about Charlie. That's the best thing about dogs, real dogs. They never judge. In that way, dogs are better than humans. Then I had a terrible thought, *What if Gina died in the hospital and the last thing I'd said to her had been a lie?* I would never be able to forgive myself. Plus, I would definitely be going straight to hell, baptized or not.

I petted Charlie some more and thought about Lyle's dog, Belinda, and then I thought about Lyle in the hospital and his dad dying from drunk-driving. What would Lyle do? He would tell Gina the truth, that's what. She would find out eventually anyways, and I would only be in worse trouble later on if I kept lying. I had to tell her. Today. This morning.

I stared at the ceiling for a minute because you should always reflect on major decisions before taking action. Then I got dressed and put Charlie in my pocket and went to use the payphone in the motel lobby so I wouldn't wake Meredith up by using the phone in our room.

Gina picked up on the first ring. She sounded pissed.

"Hi, Gina," I said.

"Tucker. Where are you?"

"Right now?"

"Yes, right now. Bright Light called. You're missing."

"Oh."

"You're a missing person, Tucker."

"Huh."

"Do you have any idea what kind of position this puts me in?"

"I'm sorry."

"And you lied to me."

"I'm really sorry."

"Tell me where you are, Tucker."

"Right now ... ?"

"Yes, right now."

"Right now I'm at the Motel Blue."

"In Toronto?"

"In Albuquerque."

"*What?*"

"Albuquerque?"

"What the hell are you doing in Albuquerque?"

"I ... I'm going to Los Angeles to find Sam Malone."

Gina said nothing. I could feel her disappointment through the phone. Her silence was like a loudspeaker next to my ear. She was screaming at me with silence.

"Gina?"

Nothing.

"Gina, I'm *sorry*."

It was like the line had gone dead except I could still hear background noise, her TV was on, she was watching *The Price Is Right*, and I could hear her heart monitor beeping.

"Gina?"

No answer.

"Gina, I'm really sorry, but you would never tell me about my father and so ... "

Then I realized what had happened. She had probably fallen into a sleep attack because of her narcolepsy. That had happened once before when she got really, really mad at me for going swimming alone at night and not telling anybody. She was right in the middle of tearing me a new one, and then she just fell asleep. Hit her head on the side of the couch on the way down.

I've figured out over the years that Gina gets her sleep attacks when she's experiencing an intense emotion. I mean, emotions aren't the only reason she falls asleep; she usually falls asleep if she's doing something passive and sitting down, like watching a movie or going to a baseball game or driving. She'll just conk out. And sometimes, when she gets angry and upset or really sad, she'll conk out too. But when she gets the cataplectic sleep attacks from feeling something too strong, that's when she can still hear and see everything, but not move. I think it must be like being trapped inside your own body.

I slowly put the phone back on its hook and decided to call her back later, after she'd had time to cool off a bit. From the sound of her voice, I could tell I was going to be grounded for at least a year. Maybe two. Maybe for the rest of my life. Maybe even longer than that. Grounded for all eternity, that's what I was going to be. But I knew it would be worth it. When I found my father, I knew it would all be worth it.

After I hung up, I went outside to see what Albuquerque looked like in the day time. The land was red and the sky was blue, and in the sky were dozens of hot-air balloons, just floating casually along as if they belonged there. One balloon was shaped like Bart Simpson. One was a big pink heart. There was a black and white striped balloon, a yellow balloon with red polka dots, a black balloon with green thunderbolts on it, and a blue balloon with yellow stars on it. There was a rainbow balloon, a balloon with a panda bear on it, one with the American flag, and a bunch more. It made my heart lift to see them all floating up, up, and away like that, and I got the feeling that maybe everything would be okay after all. Maybe every little thing would work out just the way it was meant to. Then, I swear to you, the Bart Simpson balloon winked at me. He actually winked. I know how crazy that sounds, but that's how it happened. I was kind of freaked out, so I went back inside and ran up to the room to see if Meredith was awake yet. She was all washed and packed and ready to go.

"Do you think we'll make it to California today?" Meredith said.

"I don't know. Maybe."

"Well, are you ready?"

"Just about," I said. I waited for Meredith to turn around before I took Charlie out of my pocket and put him back in my shoebox. Not because I was embarrassed or ashamed of having a little plastic dog that I talked to and sometimes petted, but because some things just hold their specialness better if you keep them to yourself.

I washed my face and brushed my teeth because I didn't know when I would get another chance to do that. I decided not to tell Meredith that Bright Light had reported us and that we were now officially missing persons. I didn't want her to worry and I especially didn't want her to say that we had to go back to Niagara Falls. Besides, how much trouble could she really get in? Both of her parents were dead.

Meredith and I left the Motel Blue and went down the street to a convenience store. We bought muffins and ate in front of the store. Meredith smoked a cigarette as she finished her coffee.

"Oh my God," Meredith said. She put her coffee down beside her.

"What?"

"It's moving."

I looked at her belly. She grabbed my hand and put it up under her shirt on her stomach. It felt hard like a watermelon.

"Feel that?"

I didn't feel anything. I shook my head.

"Wait."

I waited with my hand on her belly. Nothing happened. People came in and out of the store, and I felt weird standing there with my hand up a girl's shirt. I started to pull my hand away, but Meredith held it there.

"Hold on," she said. "There! Did you feel that?"

It was the tiniest little tap from inside. But I had felt it. There was someone in there. "Yeah," I said. We smiled at each other, and she let go of my hand.

"Amazing," Meredith said. She was grinning like she had just won the lottery.

Then a Volkswagen van pulled up in front of the store. It was painted purple with big white flowers and green leaves and a big orange peace sign on the side. Two hippies got out and they smiled big at us and the girl said, "Hey, dudes." The man-hippie had long hair and wore a billowy white shirt with brown corduroy bellbottoms. The lady-hippie wore a long green skirt and a T-shirt that said NO NUKES. Nukes can mean microwaves or nuclear bombs and since I didn't know why anyone wouldn't want a microwave, I figured she must mean no nuclear bombs. Nuclear bombs are the worst kind of bombs in the world because they kill everything for a squillion miles around, but they make an awesome mushroom cloud when they blow up, so presidents sometimes drop them just because they can. I'm not sure if Canada has any nuclear bombs. I think the United States has most of them. I'm not sure which other countries have them.

When the hippies came out of the store, Meredith asked them were they were headed.

"Sedona, Arizona," said the man.

"We're going to experience the vortexes!" said the lady. Her eyes were the same bright blue as a Slush Puppie.

"That's west of here, right?" Meredith said.

"That's right," the man said.

"Do you think we could catch a ride with you?" Meredith said.

"Sure, man. Hop in!" he said. "Always room for more in the eggplant!" Then he looked at the lady, to make sure it was all right with her, I guess, and she nodded and then he slid the side door open for us and we climbed into the van.

# 19

I think he called the van the eggplant because it was purple. I've never had eggplant before, but I know what they are—vegetables that look like an internal organ—and nobody really likes to eat them. The man-hippie's name was River and the lady-hippie's name was Poppy, and they were really, really nice to us. They had a whole kitchen in the back of their van, with pots and pans and a little stove and sink and a small table and couches and curtains and everything. It was like a tiny little home on wheels. The curtains were tie-dyed and there were glow-in-the-dark stars stuck to the roof and walls, and there were little tie-dyed pillows on the bench-couches. Maybe when I'm old enough to get my license, Gina and I should get an eggplant, then we wouldn't have to stay in crap-hat motels all the time. We could go wherever we wanted to, and our home would always be with us. Like snails. Or turtles.

Poppy drove and River made us grilled cheese sandwiches with bread that had a lot of seeds and nuts in it and thick slabs of white cheese that smelled like gym socks but was actually really good. After we ate, Meredith said she needed a nap. River gave her a blue and yellow blanket with suns and moons and stars all over it and Meredith curled up like a cat and put her Walkman on and closed her eyes. Then River smiled at me and said, "You got everything you need, kid?" and I said, "Yes, thank you." And he said, "Cool." Then he moved up front to sit beside Poppy. He smiled at her and she touched the back of his neck, and you could tell they were in love by the way their eyes shone brighter when they looked at each other.

They played a mix-tape of the Grateful Dead and Bob Dylan and Joni Mitchell and Neil Young and all that old stuff. River rolled a joint and they smoked it for a bit, and then River passed it back to me.

I took it from him and took a tiny puff. Then I coughed about a thousand times. I handed it back. Poppy and River were laughing, but not in a mean way. Then I laughed a little bit too and felt kind of sparkly inside.

I opened the tie-dyed curtains and watched the world go by for a while. All the grass and rocks and dirt looked dried out and sunburned. The sky was a great wide ocean that no one would ever drown in. I thought about how it's kind of funny that people are still being hippies in 1992 when everyone knows that hippies were really just a fad in the sixties. Hanging out with hippies is kind of like stepping into a time machine. But it's a time machine that only goes backward.

Gina had a dancer friend in Vancouver named Lucy who always wore hippie costumes. She had a long blonde wig that went down to her bum and flower crowns and peace sign necklaces. Lucy was nice. She used to tell me I was the luckiest kid in the world to have Gina as a mom. And she would always kiss Gina on the lips whenever she saw her. I think maybe Lucy and Gina were best friends.

I must have dozed off for a while, but I woke up suddenly because Poppy was swerving the eggplant all over the freeway. She screamed as gravel spat out from the tires and we came to a bumpy stop on the shoulder.

Meredith sat up and took out her earphones. "What is it? What happened?"

Poppy was crying and River tried to comfort her, but she swatted his hand away and was pretty much going ballistic. "I hit it! I hit it! I killed it!"

"Killed what?" Meredith said.

"A rabbit," River said.

"Oh," Meredith said. Her eyes welled up with tears. Probably because she had just finished reading *Watership Down*. Or maybe because she had the pregnancy hormones that make you cry when you don't want to. Or maybe Meredith welled up because Poppy was having a freak-out of epic proportions and it was scary to watch.

Poppy pulled at her hair and rammed her head against the glass window; she ripped apart the beaded curtain and strings of beads flew around the van, pinging off every surface. She put her face into a pillow and screamed and screamed and screamed. River just stared out the windshield and watched the traffic whiz by. Finally spent, Poppy collapsed in a heap and put her head in River's lap and sobbed. He smoothed her long hair and said, "Death is just a part of life, babe. Everything is meant to die sometime. That was its time."

"We have to bury it," Poppy said, looking up. Her electric blue eyes shone like a neon sign.

"Babe, we can't bury it. It's in the middle of the road. And we have to meet our shaman at seven."

Poppy got out of the van and walked into the oncoming traffic like she wasn't even afraid to be hit. She scooped up the rabbit in her skirt and carried it back to the van. The rabbit wasn't very big. It was pale brown and its legs were all mangled and bent at odd angles, its face and ears were bloody, and its stomach was split open and parts of its intestines were falling out. Meredith got out and barfed into the burnt grass.

"We need a box," Poppy said.

"Seriously? We're going to do this right now?" River said.

Poppy gave him a look.

"All right, all right," River said. "A box?" he began looking through the glove compartment. "How about a napkin?"

"NO! We have to give him a proper burial."

"Pops ... "

"We. Are. Burying. This. Rabbit."

River sighed and came into the back of the van. He opened drawers and shuffled through cutlery, ropes, plastic bags. He held up a plastic bag. "Does it *have* to be a box?"

"YES!" Poppy yelled. She cradled the rabbit in the folds of her skirt as if she could bring it back to life by rocking it back and forth.

"I have a box," I said.

"You do?" River looked at me like I'd just agreed to give him my kidney.

"Yep." I opened my backpack and took out my shoebox. I don't know why I had hesitated to offer it. It was just an old Converse box, nothing special. It was the stuff *inside* it that was special. I had gotten that mixed up for a minute. "Can I have that bag?"

River handed me the plastic bag, and I dumped the stuff from the box into it and then twisted it up and tied it in a knot and put it into my backpack. I handed the shoebox to River.

"Thanks, Tucker," Poppy said.

"No problem," I said.

River handed my box to Poppy and she carefully settled the rabbit into it. River grabbed a small shovel and we all marched about fifty feet away from the road in a little procession. Poppy led the way, then Meredith, then me, then River.

"Watch out for snakes!" River yelled.

Meredith screamed.

"Don't worry. They're more scared of you than you are of them," he said.

"How can you possibly know that?" Meredith said.

River never answered. Poppy paced around a bit, "to feel the energetic resonance of the earth," she said. Finally, she found a spot she was happy with, and River began to dig a shallow grave in the desert.

Then Poppy lowered in my Converse box that I'd had for as long as I could remember. Tears streamed down her face. "This here was a good rabbit," Poppy said. "A strong rabbit. A fast rabbit. He had many friends, many family members, and he will be missed. Goddess bless this rabbit as he travels to the next realm." Then she whispered, "I'm so sorry." She took off one of her earrings and placed it on top of the box.

River rubbed her back a little bit and brought her into his body for a sideways hug. Then Meredith bent down and took a safety-pin off her shoelace that had three coloured beads on it and put it on top of the box. River scratched his forehead and took off the green bandana he was wearing and dropped that into the rabbit's grave. I didn't have anything in my pockets except an elastic band so I threw that in. River looked at me and nodded and then began covering the shoebox with dirt. We all stood silently while he finished and then for a few more seconds after he was done.

"Okay?" River said, looking at Poppy.

"Wait!" she said, then took off running into the desert.

"Snakes!" he called.

"I *know!*" she yelled back.

When Poppy returned, she had a small bouquet of wildflowers. Yellow and purple. She laid them over the grave and gave the stems a pat. "There," she said.

"Okay," River said, and held out his hand to help her up.

"Thank you, River," Poppy said. "And thank *you* guys," she said and pulled us in close and the four of us had a group-hug. I was squished against Poppy's armpit, but it wasn't so bad. She smelled like tea and spices and honey and orange peels all mixed together. "Mmm," she said. Then she released us from the hug. She brushed away the hair that had fallen across her face. "Well, I guess we'd better keep on truckin'," she said. "Would you mind driving now, River? I'm still a little shaky." She held out her hand, and it was vibrating.

"Yeah, of course," he said. They walked back to the eggplant holding hands. Meredith and I trailed behind. I looked at cactuses, and Meredith smoked part of a cigarette. I picked a little yellow flower. Usually when I pick flowers I give them to Gina, but since she wasn't there, I gave it to Meredith.

"You're sweet, kid," she said, and tucked it behind her ear.

Poppy and River stopped at a gas station in Flagstaff since it would be easier for us to keep heading west from there. River washed the windshield and Meredith went inside the store.

"I hope you find what you're looking for," Poppy said to me.

"Thanks," I said. "You too. With the vortexes."

She smiled. "Here," she said, taking off one of her hemp bracelets. "I want you to have this." She tied it around my wrist and the blue and green beads woven into it sparkled in the sunlight.

"Thanks," I said. "I've never had a bracelet before."

Then Meredith came out and River put the squeegee away. We all stood in a little clump beside the eggplant.

"Thank you guys so much for the ride and lunch and everything," Meredith said.

Poppy gave Meredith a hug and River gave me a hug and then they switched. While she hugged me, Poppy whispered in my ear, "Stay gold, Ponyboy." And I didn't know what she meant, but it made me happy. A little bit of Poppy's sweet-tea BO clung to my clothes so that long after she and River had jumped into the van and waved their arms out the windows so that their arms looked like wings flying the eggplant away, I could still smell her.

# 20

Meredith and I were hot and dusty so we hung around the gas station for a while and washed our hair in the sink and drank a bunch of water and got submarine sandwiches.

Two vultures soared in a circle high above the gas station. I called Gina again. No one answered. I felt a little sick to my stomach. What if she had gotten worse? Or gone into a coma? What if she had *died?* I tried the number again. Nothing. And there was nothing I could do about it. Her not answering could mean a lot of things, but one thing it definitely *did* mean was that it was more important for me to find my father now than it had ever been before.

Meredith came out of the store then, all panicky. "Tucker, something bad just happened."

"What?"

"I was in the bathroom, okay, and I put my purse beside the sink and then turned around for like, *two seconds*, to grab a paper-towel, and when I turned around again, it was gone."

"Just now?"

She nodded. "Did you see anyone come out of the store with it?"

"No."

"I can't believe this," she said.

"Maybe the person who took it is still in the store."

We ran into the gas station. Everybody looked suspicious, but nobody had Meredith's purse or a bag big enough to be holding it. Meredith and I were the only people in the store with backpacks. I went into the men's washroom. No one was in there. I kicked the doors of all the stalls open. Her purse wasn't in any of them or in the garbage can. I ran outside and around to the back parking lot and checked behind the bushes and in the dumpster. Then I went and looked at all the people getting gas and even asked one lady if she had seen anybody with a little green purse come out of the store, but nobody knew anything. Meredith sat against the brick wall, her backpack beside her. She was drinking an iced tea, and when I sat down beside her she handed me a Coke.

"Thanks," I said.

"Yeah."

"I'm sorry about your purse. That really sucks."

"I can't believe it. Everything I had was in there. My wallet, my money, my ID ... "

"At least you still have your backpack," I said.

"Yeah, I have clothes. Great."

I took a long drink of my Coke. It was ice cold.

"You still have money left?" she said.

"Yeah."

"How much?"

"Don't worry. I have enough for both of us."

She sighed and started peeling off the label on her iced tea. A bad thought came into my brain then and I tried to shove it out, but it stayed put. "What?" Meredith said. "Why are you looking at me like that?"

"Like what?"

"Like that. You're looking at me weird."

"No I'm not," I said.

"You are."

I looked away and watched a family with ten kids climb out of a big white van.

Meredith narrowed her eyes at me. "What? You think I made it up? You think I just *said* my purse got stolen so you would have to pay for the rest of the trip?"

I shrugged.

"Are you for real right now?"

"How did you buy these drinks if you didn't have your wallet?" I said.

"I had money in my pocket. Jesus Christ, Tucker. Thanks a lot. Talk about trusting someone ..."

"You stole Chad's car," I mumbled.

"Yeah, okay. I stole Chad's car, all right. I stole Chad's car so that *you* could get your stupid father fantasy over and done with and fucking *grow up already!*"

"Whatever," I said.

"This is bullshit," she said as she stood up. "This is the biggest bunch of bullshit that ever was. This whole trip is total bullshit. It's fucking ridiculous. I don't even know why I'm here. I don't even know why we're doing this." She clutched her forehead like her brain was about to burst through her skull.

"We're going to find my father, Sam Malone," I said.

"Your father is *not* Sam Malone, you idiot. Sam Malone doesn't even exist!"

I stood up. "Shut up. You don't know anything about my father."

"I know he's not some stupid character in some stupid TV show."

"Sam Malone's not stupid!"

"Are you brain dead? There *is* no one named Sam Malone! He's an actor! His name is Ted Danson!"

"But he's ... he's based on someone real. Someone exactly like that in real life."

She shook her head. "No he's not, you dumbass. He's based on a *character* someone made up. *Someone wrote him!* He's not real!"

"He played for the Boston Red Sox," I said.

"In the *show*. Not in real life."

"You don't know anything."

"It's just a stupid *show*, Tucker."

"*Cheers* isn't stupid."

"No, *you're* stupid. If you actually believe he's your dad, you're dumber than a bag of hammers. Either that, or you need psychiatric therapy."

"Why did you come with me then?"

"Why did I come?"

"Yeah." I wiped my nose on my sleeve. "If it's so idiotic, then why would you even come?"

She threw her hands up. "Because I wanted to get away from that shithole we live in! I wanted a change of scenery!"

"You wanted a vacation."

"Exactly. I wanted a vacation."

"An all-expenses-paid vacation," I said.

She shook her head and shot death-lasers into me with her eyes.

"Well," I said. "How is it?"

"How's my vacation?"

"Yeah."

She shrugged. "The weather's here, wish you were great."

It felt like a billion paper-cuts sliced into me all at once and then she dumped a bucket of lemon juice over my head. "You know what, Meredith?"

"What?" she stood with her hands on her hips.

"You're an asshole."

"At least I'm not delusional." She spat onto the sidewalk.

I turned and speed-walked away. I didn't know where I was going, I didn't know which direction I was headed, I didn't know what road I was on. All I knew was that I needed to get away from her.

\*\*\*

I ran across the freeway and walked and walked and clenched and unclenched my fists and felt my face and neck turn red. The world felt too hot and everything was stupid. After a while, I came to a Texaco. I bought another Coke and drank it and felt a teeny bit better. Then I didn't know what else to do so I went to the payphone around the side of the gas station and tried Gina again.

"Tucker?" she picked up on the first ring.

"Hi," I said.

"Don't hang up."

"Okay."

"I want to know exactly where you are and who you're with and then you're turning your little butt around and coming straight back to Niagara Falls. Do not pass go, do not collect two hundred dollars. Do you understand me, mister?"

"I'm in Flagstaff, Arizona."

"Where exactly?"

"At a Texaco."

"I'm sending the police to come get you."

"No! Don't!"

"What else am I supposed to do, Tucker? You tell me."

"I just need a few more days. We're almost there."

"Who are you with?"

"Meredith. But she's—"

"Is that this Mary person you told me about?"

"Yes."

"From the group home?"

"Yes."

"How old is Meredith?"

"Sixteen."

"What in hell are you doing, Tucker James? Are you trying to give me a heart attack?"

"No. I'm trying to get to Los Angeles."

"You don't need to go to Los Angeles, Tucker."

"Yes. I. Do."

"*Why?*"

"Because you won't tell me anything about my father!" I yelled into the phone. Tears prickled my eyes. "For eleven years, I've been asking you about him and you won't tell me a goddamned thing." I wiped my nose on the back of my hand.

"Tucker—"

"*What?*"

"If you come home right now, I promise to tell you all about him."

"Everything?"

"Everything."

"Tell me now."

"I ... I can't. It has to be in person."

"Why?"

"It's not the kind of thing you tell someone over the phone," she said.

"Well, I have to go anyways," I said.

"Your father is not in Los Angeles, Tucker."

"You don't know that!"

"I'm pretty sure."

"He probably is! The bartender in Boston told me."

Gina began to cry. "Please come home, Tucker. I need you here with me. I need to know you're safe."

"Right after I go to Hollywood, I'll come back. Promise."

"Let me talk to Meredith," she said.

"She can't come to the phone right now," I said. I didn't even know if I'd ever see Meredith again, and a small seizure ripped through my heart.

Gina was quiet for a minute. "I didn't think you'd do this to me. Not yet, at least."

I didn't know what to say so I didn't say anything.

"I'm getting out in a few days," she said.

"That's good," I said. "That's really good."

"I'll need a cane for a while, but not forever."

I tried to picture Gina with a cane. But all that came to me was Mr. Peanut. How would she dance with a cane? If she couldn't dance, what would she do for money? But I knew I shouldn't ask her that now. She was upset enough already and I didn't want to give her another sleep attack. There was really nothing left to say. I wasn't coming home, and she couldn't do anything to make me. In chess they call that a stalemate. That's what Gina and I were having. A stalemate over the phone.

"I can come and get you," she said. "I'll leave right now."

"No, don't," I said. "I'm okay. Everything's okay, and I'm going to Los Angeles. Besides, you can't even drive."

"I'll take the bus," she said.

"I'll be back home by the time your bus gets here," I said.

"How are you getting to L.A.?" she asked.

"People give us rides," I said.

"Oh good Christ," she said. "Tucker—"

"They're nice people. Really good people."

"Tucker, *Jesus!*"

"What?"

"Don't you know what people do to children who hitchhike?"

"No."

"They *take* them. They steal them and do bad things to them. Sometimes they kill them. Do you realize how dangerous it is to be doing what you're doing? You could be killed. I might never see you again!" Her voice broke, and I could hear her blow her nose in the background.

"We only take rides from regular people," I said. "No weirdos."

"You don't know who's weird and who's not! You don't *know!*"

"Meredith knows."

"Meredith doesn't know."

"She gets feelings."

Gina started crying again. I wanted to tell her about Sherry and her fat baby and Lyle and Belinda the golden retriever and Timothy and the quiet man and Stacey and Camden and Hal and Chris and Dylan and Eric and Poppy and River, but I didn't know what to say except that they hadn't hurt us or killed us and some of them had even made us sandwiches and given us gummy worms and ice cold Cokes and bracelets. But I didn't think it would make Gina feel any better so I just said, "People are usually good."

"Can you take the bus the rest of the way? Can you please, *please* take the bus?"

I didn't say anything.

"Tucker?"

"I don't know," I said, which was the truth. But I knew that I wouldn't, because the bus takes forever and rides are fast and I was so close to finding him that I couldn't stop or even slow down.

"You need to take the bus, Tucker. Do you have enough money? I can wire you some money."

"I have enough," I said.

"And you and Meredith have to stick together," Gina said. "It's safer that way. Don't get split up no matter what."

"Okay," I said. "I have to go now."

"I love you, Tucker. Be safe. Be careful. I am so mad at you right now but I want you to know that I love you more than anything in the world."

"Okay," I said.

"Call me tomorrow," she said. "First thing."

"All right. Bye, Gina."

"Bye, lamb chop." Her voice caught in her throat and I knew that after we hung up she would bawl her eyes out, but in a way, it was her own fault for not telling me about my father.

I sat down on the concrete and leaned my back against the brick wall of the store and felt like a pile of horse manure. Meredith and I were split up, Gina didn't think my father was in Los Angeles, and I wasn't sure about anything anymore. I watched a line of army ants crawling around my shoe and thought about how messed up everything had gotten. *What would Lyle do?* I wondered. I watched the ants for a long time. Even though people were coming into the gas station who could probably give me a ride, I didn't ask anyone. I didn't even look up. I just wanted to watch the ants. The ants were busy. They knew exactly what they were doing and where they were going and what they were supposed to do when they got there. They didn't have to wonder about anything.

Then I heard someone whistle and I looked up and Meredith was standing beside a really tall black woman who was pumping gas into a yellow Mustang convertible. Meredith waved me over.

I stood up carefully so as not to crush any of the ants and walked over to Meredith and the tall lady.

"Tucker," Meredith said, "this is Dee."

The lady stuck out her hand for me to shake. "Pleasure to meet you, Tucker." Dee said in a scratchy voice. Her hand was a giant's hand. She had puffed up dark-blonde hair and wore a sequined head-band with two pink flamingoes on it. Her eyelashes were so long that I knew they were fake because no one in the world actually has eyelashes that long, even in the Guinness Book.

I looked at Meredith.

"Listen, about before ..." Meredith said.

"I'll just use the ladies' room," Dee said, putting the gas nozzle back on its hook. "Back in a jiff."

Meredith reached into her backpack. "I found my purse." She held it up.

I nodded and bit my lip.

"Somebody gave it to the cashier. Said she just found it in the bathroom."

"Was everything still in it?"

"Yeah," she said. "Even the money. I couldn't believe it."

"I told you. People are usually good."

"Maybe," she shrugged.

"So, do you still want to come to L.A. with me?" I said.

She nodded.

"Even though it's stupid?"

"There are stupider things I could be doing," she said.

"That's good because it's safer if we stick together."

Her mouth curled up on one side. "You didn't think you could get rid of me that easily, did you?"

Then Dee came back smiling and hopped into her convertible without even opening the door. "This is my car, Limón," Dee said.

"Hi, Limón," I said. Even though I had just said hi to a car and I knew that was beyond dumb, I didn't even care because I was getting to ride in a *convertible!*

"Dee's going to Vegas," Meredith said, climbing in the back.

"That's right, sweetie. But I'm making a little pit-stop along the way." Dee pulled onto the freeway.

"Where?" I said.

"The Grand Canyon," Dee said and bounced up and down in her seat.

I wished that we weren't stopping at the Grand Canyon since it was just a stupid hole in the ground, and I wanted to get to L.A. as soon as possible. But you don't pass up good rides because you never know when the next one is going to come along.

I watched Dee as she drove. I looked at her face and her hands. Her jaw was sharp and boxy, and her hands were like baseball mitts. I liked being in a convertible and I liked the feeling of the wind rushing through my hair, but I got kind of squirmy and my stomach felt weird when I realized that I wasn't totally sure if Dee was a real lady or not. But I didn't know why any man would *want* to be a woman since being a man was so much easier. I snuck a few looks at her boobs and they looked big and round and squishable like nice boobs do.

"Dee," I said.

"Yeah, honey?" She turned to me, smiling, her pink lipstick glimmering in the sunlight.

"Are you a man or a woman?"

"Tucker!" Meredith kicked the back of my seat, hard.

"Oh, it's okay," Dee glanced back at Meredith, then turned to me. If you looked past her two-foot eyelashes, her eyes were sad and serious. She cleared her throat. "I was born a man, but I feel like a woman inside."

"Oh," I said.

"So sometimes I dress like a woman."

"Even though you're really a man?" I said.

"That's right," she said.

"How do you decide?"

"Decide what, sugar?"

"When you'll be a man and when you'll be a woman?"

She smiled and winked at Meredith in the rear-view mirror. "Well, where I grew up, where I *live*, there's really no one like me."

"There's no one like anyone," I said.

"That's true," Dee said. "But what I mean is, people who are one way on the outside but feel the other way on the inside."

"Oh," I said.

"So, in Sweetwater, I always present as a man. But if I'm going away or when I'm alone, if I know I'm going to be alone for a while, then I can let my inside self show, and I can dress as a woman. Dress in drag."

"What's drag?" I said.

"Tucker, just shut up. Leave her alone," Meredith said.

"It's all right, sweetheart. I don't mind."

"Do you mind if I smoke?" Meredith asked.

"Oh sure, just make sure you roll the window down." Dee laughed and slapped her thigh. "What was I saying?"

"Drag."

"Oh yes. Well, drag is actually a word from Shakespeare's time. You know William Shakespeare, the playwright?"

"Not personally," I said.

Dee laughed. She had a big cackly laugh that was contagious. "Well, in Shakespeare's time, women couldn't act on stage, they weren't allowed to, so all the female parts had to be played by men, so there would be a little note next to the actor's name that was supposed to play a woman, and it would say, *Dressed As Girl*, and that's where the term drag came from, D.R.A.G. Get it?"

I nodded.

The person sitting next to me was a man dressed as a woman who felt like a woman on the inside but was actually a man on the outside so had to go in disguise to be what she really was. I felt a little weird about it all, but not as weird as I had felt a few minutes before when I didn't know. And the longer we drove with Dee, the less weird I felt. Dee was Dee. It didn't really matter if she was a man or a woman. She was funny and nice and liked to sing and laugh and chew Hubba Bubba and blow big bubbles that popped all over her face.

At first I'd been nervous that maybe Dee was one of the weirdos that Gina had warned me about. But after about half an hour, I knew that Dee was not one of those weirdos. Even though she was different, she was just like everybody else. She wanted people to like her. She wanted people to see her for who she really was inside. I started to understand what Meredith meant about feelings she gets about people. But, I think for me, it wasn't the feeling I got *about* a person, it was how the person made me feel about *myself*. Dee made me feel kind of ... *fabulous*.

# 21

Before long, we were entering Grand Canyon National Park. Dee paid the toll and drove to the visitor centre. Then she parked Limón and we walked to the lookout point.

"Whoa," I said, leaning over the edge of the cliff to get a better look.

Meredith didn't say anything but came up beside me and stood so close to me, I could feel the heat from her skin. The three of us looked out over the abyss.

"Isn't it *magnificent?*" Dee said. "I've always been in such a hurry to get to Vegas. This is the first time I've stopped here."

"How often do you go to Vegas?" Meredith asked her.

"Oh, as often as I can. Las Vegas is the one place I really feel like I can be myself, know what I mean?"

I nodded, even though I felt like myself pretty much everywhere I went.

"I'd like to move there, eventually," she sighed. "It takes a while to figure all that out, though."

I didn't see what there was to figure out. When Gina and I wanted to move, we packed up all our junk and caught the next bus out of town. Moving is easy. Staying in one place is hard.

"I'm going to go find the ladies' room," Dee said. "Will you kitties be all right here for a minute?"

"Yep," I said.

Dee left and I looked over at Meredith. She had a sad-worried look on her face. "What's wrong?" I said.

"I'm the Grand Canyon," she said quietly.

"Um, *no* ... you're Meredith."

"I feel like that," she said, pointing to the centre of the rocky pit.

"I feel like there's this big, gaping hole inside me and it's been there for a million years and it'll be there for a million more, and nothing will ever be able to fill it up. Ever. And everyone can see it. Everybody knows it's there."

I stared at her.

"It's like everything bad that's ever happened to me has dug a little scoop out, and so now I'm almost completely hollowed out. I'm the Grand Canyon, and there's nothing I can do about it." She wrapped her arms around herself.

"What about the good things that happen to you?" I said. "Don't they fill it in a little?"

She shrugged.

"What do you think would happen if you hooked Niagara Falls up to the Grand Canyon?" I said.

"You couldn't do that. No one could do that."

"Yeah, but say you could," I said. "One million bathtubs of water a second, pouring into the biggest bathtub in the world." I held out my arms, taking in the gigantic crater before us.

"It would fill up eventually, I guess," Meredith said.

"Exactly," I said.

"Exactly *what?*"

"If you're the Grand Canyon, then I'm Niagara Falls."

Meredith looked at me like I had three heads. Then her face cracked into a smile. "Okay," she said.

"Okay?"

She nodded and wiped her eyes on the sleeve of her hoodie.

Then I gave her a hug because it seemed like the best thing to do at the time. Her body felt soft and warm against mine and a piece of her hair tickled my nose.

"I'm sorry, Tucker," she murmured into the side of my neck.

"I know," I said.

Then Dee ran up to us and said, "Ooh, ooh, me too!" and she encircled both of us in a hug. I could feel her thick arm muscles and the slippery material of her tube-top against my skin. Then I thought about how everyone has little Grand Canyons inside them, but everyone has little Niagara Fallses too.

\*\*\*

Dee decided that she liked the Grand Canyon so much that she wanted to stay and do the sunset horseback riding tour. She apologized all over the place for not taking us straight to Las Vegas, but she said that she couldn't have foreseen the power that the Grand Canyon would have over her and that she knew we would understand.

"I'm sure you can find a ride here with someone," she said. "I know you will. But on the off-chance you don't, I'll be back a little after sunset and we can go then. I'm so sorry, darlings. Do you hate me? You must."

"It's okay," I said. "It's no problem." Even though it *was* kind of a problem, but what could I say? I couldn't tell Dee what to do. I couldn't tell her not to go horseback riding at sunset in the Grand Canyon. *I* wanted to go horseback riding at sunset in the Grand Canyon. But even more than that, I wanted to get to Los Angeles.

We said goodbye to Dee, and she hugged both of us again and gave us butterfly kisses with her ridiculous eyelashes.

"Good luck," she said.

"You too," I said.

"Look me up if you ever come through Sweetwater, Texas."

"I will," I said. But I knew I never would. I wouldn't even know how to find her since she'd probably be listed under her man-name in the phonebook.

Meredith and I hung around the parking lot, scouting for a ride. Finally, after about six or seven unsuccessful attempts, Meredith found a dark-haired woman wearing a blue dress who said she could take us to Las Vegas.

The woman's name was Lorena and she drove a silver Ford Taurus, which was a rental car. She looked as if she had been crying. Lorena had a Spanish accent and didn't play any music in the car. Meredith sat shotgun and I leaned my head against the back window, breathing in the new-car smell. The new-car smell is gross but somehow comforting at the same time. We drove for a while, and no one said anything. Lorena kept sniffling, and I wished that I had a Kleenex I could give her. I watched all the orange and pink rocks go by. The sun in Arizona is redder than anywhere else I've been. It hung low over the mountains and throbbed like a beating heart, bleeding red across the sky.

"What brings you to Las Vegas?" Meredith finally asked.

Lorena's jaw clenched. "My husband wanted to take me on a trip. A romantic weekend getaway, he called it. We've been having some problems," she turned to Meredith. "You know ..."

Meredith nodded.

"So, anyways, he gets me all excited about this trip, this *romantic weekend getaway*. I bring all these special outfits, I plan this trip to the Grand Canyon for us. We were going to have a picnic up there, watch the sunset. I got champagne. I got havarti. That's his favourite, havarti. But, here I am. Alone. *Why?* Because he's up all night playing fucking *blackjack*, and too tired to come out to the Grand Canyon today, that's why."

"That's shitty," Meredith said.

"You're goddamn right it's shitty! Who has a romantic picnic all by themselves? No one, that's who! He's the biggest mistake I've ever made in my life." Lorena choked back a sob and then began to cry.

"I'm sorry," Meredith said.

"You don't need to be sorry. *He's* the one who should say sorry!" Meredith nodded.

"But he won't. He won't say it. He never apologizes for anything. *Nada.*" Lorena wiped her nose on the back of her hand and gripped the steering wheel. She blew out her breath and the air lifted up her bangs. "Sometimes, I just want to chop his dick off and throw it out the window, you know what I mean?"

"Yeah," Meredith said. "Totally."

I squirmed in the backseat and pressed my legs together. Lorena was a small, sweet looking lady, but you could tell that on the inside, she held a rage.

I wondered what Gina was doing. This was the longest I'd ever been away from Gina, and I missed her, but I knew that I was doing the right thing. I couldn't go my whole life without meeting my father. It was dangerous, what Meredith and I were doing, I knew Gina was right about that, but there were other ways of living that were dangerous, too. I would be twelve soon and then I would be thirteen. And everyone knows what happens to teenage boys who don't know who their father is.

\*\*\*

Finally, we came to the top of a hill, and I could see the city of Las Vegas shining below. It was alive with lights. When I closed my eyes I could still see them.

"Where do you want me to let you off?" Lorena said.

"You can just drop us at any of these motels," Meredith said.

We drove by one with a fifty-foot neon pink flamingo on the outside of it. I remembered Dee's headband. "That one," I said. "The Pink Flamingo."

Lorena pulled over.

"Thanks for the ride," Meredith said. "I hope things get better with your husband. I'm sure they will."

"Either things will get better or things will end," she said. "Either way ... it will eventually be better." She turned and smiled at me. "Hey, thanks for listening, you guys. Really. No one ever really listens to me at home. People can be so ... you know."

I nodded, although I didn't know. People were people. They could be so many different things.

"Bye, Lorena," I said, getting out of the car.

"*Vaya con Dios, angelitos*," she said, and gave us a small wave as she pulled away.

We checked in at the front desk, but they didn't have any rooms left with two beds.

I turned to Meredith. "What do you think?"

She shrugged. "It doesn't matter," she said. "I'm so tired I could sleep in the bathtub."

The first thing I did when we got to our room was check the nightstand for the Gideon bible. It was there. Then both of us brushed our teeth and got into bed with our clothes on. We were too tired to even watch TV. But it turns out that Las Vegas is the worst place in the world to fall asleep because:

1. All the lights are so bright

2. People are partying and yelling and singing and talking and burping and playing music

3. You might have to share a bed with a girl

I crunched myself all the way over to the very edge of the bed so that I wouldn't disturb Meredith or touch her by accident because I didn't want her to think that I'd touched her on purpose and was trying to get to first base with her or something stupid like that. Between that and the noise and the lights, I basically didn't sleep a wink all night.

Staying up all night is okay when you *mean* to do it, then it can be pretty fun, but when you actually *want* to sleep and you can't, it really, really, sucks. Every hour seems so long. Eventually you just want it to be morning already so you can stop trying to sleep and just get up and have the worst day of your life.

# 22

When the blue light of dawn glowed through our window, I gave up trying to sleep and got up to go see what Las Vegas was all about and find something to eat.

I saw a woman asleep in a doorway wearing only a bra and a skirt. I saw a haggard-looking man who shoved me and asked me a question, but I couldn't understand what he was saying. His front teeth were missing. I saw a beefy looking guy in a grey suit talking into a huge telephone that didn't have a cord. I saw a fat woman wearing a green sun visor that read Slots-A-Fun counting out change on a bus bench. I saw a redheaded guy with his arms around two pretty ladies who were wearing high, high heels. I saw a Native American guy looking in the window of a western-wear store. I saw a guy who looked just like Fabio and maybe even *was* Fabio leaning against the side of a bank. I saw an Asian woman in a black dress-suit smoking a cigarette with a cigarette-holder. I saw a guy in a dirty pinstripe suit drinking something out of a paper bag. I saw two women kissing each other. I saw a man in an Adidas track suit smashing his forehead against a brick wall, again and again. I saw a bald man with a patch over his eye. I saw someone like Dee, a D.R.A.G.

The D.R.A.G. was wearing a short silver wig and a purple sequined dress with blue, green, and gold waves up the sides. It reminded me of this dancing costume Gina bought after some guy in Vancouver tipped her 500 bucks one night. It's a sequined butterfly costume with full-length wings. She can put her arms through the slits and make the wings stretch out and the tips of the wings go all the way to the floor. She wears it only on special occasions, and when she does, she looks so glamorous I can't believe she's my mother.

I went to Denny's and ordered a Moons Over My Hammy and a

chocolate milk. After I ate, I felt better. I went back to the motel and wrapped a T-shirt around my head to block out the light. I got into bed and finally slept. When I woke up again, Meredith was leaning over me saying, "Rise and shine, monkey-butt."

# 23

The next ride we got was with Relvis. Relvis drove a Buick
Roadmaster station wagon with wood panelling on the sides. It
was loaded up with blankets and cardboard boxes and garbage
bags and smelled like a hamster cage. Relvis wore a white suit with
tassels on the sleeves because he was still in costume. Or maybe
that's how he always dressed, I'm not sure. Relvis was an Elvis
impersonator. He looked pretty much the same as Elvis except
that he had pitted acne scars on his cheeks. He wore tinted glasses
and talked out of the side of his mouth. I guess if you impersonate
someone for long enough, you eventually *become* that person. Or
at least a version of that person.

"You kids like music?" Relvis asked as he flipped through the
radio stations.

"Yeah, of course," I said. "Who doesn't like music?"

"Some people don't," he said. "I try not to associate with those
people, though."

"I like lots of different kinds of music," I said.

"I like Elvis, personally," Relvis said.

"No kidding," Meredith said.

"Don't be cruel, baby," Relvis said.

I glanced back at Meredith and she rolled her eyes.

Relvis checked her out in the rear-view mirror and jammed his
tongue into the side of his cheek. Meredith turned her head to watch
a scuffle on the street. A cop was arresting a young black guy, shoving him hard against the hood of a police cruiser. Relvis clucked his
tongue and slowed down as we passed them. He caught the eye of
the cop and pointed to his own eyes and then back to the cop.

"Is this place a hole or what?" Relvis said.

"Or what," I said.

"Huh," he said. "You don't know Vegas."

"I don't know anything. I'm eleven years old."

"And you know what?"

"What?"

"The older you get, the less you know."

"I figured."

"It's just the way it goes."

"I don't even *know* what I don't know," I said.

"That's right, kid." Relvis shut off the radio and started humming "In the Ghetto." "You want to know the truth?" he asked.

"Sure," I said.

"The truth is, I hate Vegas. I'll always be Relvis, but do I have to do it in Vegas?"

"If you don't want to live here, then you probably shouldn't live here," I said.

"That's right. That's exactly right. This damn city's killing me. That's why I'm moving. This is me moving." He gestured to his garbage in the back. "It's now or never. Time to stop talking about it and actually do it," he said.

"A little less conversation, a little more action?" Meredith said.

"You got it, sweetheart!"

Meredith and I laughed.

"I just have one small problem," Relvis said.

"What's that?" Meredith said.

"I don't know where to go."

"You could go to Canada," I said.

"Canada!" Relvis said the word *Canada* like it was a disease. "Why would anyone want to go to Canada?"

"That's where we live," Meredith said.

"Oh," Relvis said. "Sorry."

I shrugged. "It's pretty nice. And there aren't too many Elvises."

"Huh."

"Plus, we have Tim Horton's," I said.

"Who's that?"

"It's a donut shop. They have the best donuts. And they're everywhere. All over the country."

"You want some advice, kid?"

"Sure," I said.

"Keep your eye on the donut, not the hole."

I thought about that for the rest of the trip.

No one said anything for a while. Then Relvis said, "You know what, I don't think Canada's the place for me. I'm looking for something particular, and Canada ain't got it."

"What are you looking for?" I said.

"I'm looking for the American Dream," Relvis said.

"Where's that?" I said.

"I'm not sure exactly. Could be Alaska. Could be Hawaii. Could be Hackensack, New Jersey. But I'll know it when I see it," he said. "I can tell you that for sure."

***

When we stopped for gas, I called Gina from a payphone but no one answered. I was sort of relieved that I didn't have to talk to Gina because she probably had some elaborate plan all worked out where she would make me fly home that day or take a direct bus from Las Vegas or something stupid like that, that did not involve me getting to Hollywood and meeting Sam Malone. I knew it was hard on her, what I was doing, but it was hard on *me* not knowing who my father was. Gina should've thought of that one of the five billion times I'd asked her to tell me about him.

I sat in the car and waited for Relvis and Meredith to finish up in the store. I wasn't hungry or thirsty, I just wanted to get there.

They got back in the car and Relvis set a plastic bag by my feet and then we were back on the freeway. "You hungry, kid? You can have one of them candy bars." He nodded toward the bag.

"I'm okay. Thanks."

He took one and tore the wrapper open with his teeth and spit it out onto the floor. "How you doin' back there, baby girl?" He eyed Meredith in the rear-view.

"Fine," she said. "Good."

"When are you scheduled to pop?"

"A few months still," she said.

"Going to be one beautiful baby, that's for sure." He winked at her in the rear-view mirror.

Meredith stared at him for a second, then turned her head to look out the window.

"Thinking of names yet?"

"Not really."

"You could name him Relvis if you want," Relvis said. "If he's a boy. For girls, I like Priscilla and Lisa Marie."

"Yeah," Meredith said. "I'll think about it."

Then Relvis lit two cigarettes at once and smoked them both at the same time. I stared at him. He glanced over at me and shrugged. "Sometimes one just ain't enough," he said.

Meredith laughed and rolled down her window and I did too.

"Want to pick a tape, kid?"

"Sure," I said.

He opened the cover of the arm rest and there were about fifteen cassettes lined up in there. In alphabetical order. Mostly Elvis. Some Lisa Marie. Some other country stuff. I picked Johnny Cash and stuck it in the tape deck.

"Excellent choice," Relvis said, nodding. He licked his finger and smoothed his sideburns down.

The clock on the car stereo was the wrong time so I pushed the button to try to set it. But the numbers just kept going and never stopped.

Relvis shook his head. "Sometimes, things get broke and they can't ever be fixed again," he said.

I punched some more buttons but the clock numbers didn't stop. All four of them raced from zero to nine and back, again and again.

"Doesn't matter what time the clock says anyways," Relvis said. "It's only ever now."

By the time both sides of the tape had finished, Relvis had decided that he was going to drive north. Maybe even all the way to Alaska. "See if I can meet any cats as cool as you two up there," he said, grinning. He dropped us off where the I-15 intersects with the I-40 so we could keep heading west.

"I have to say it," I said, as Meredith and I got out of the car.

"Go ahead," Relvis said.

"Thank you, thank you very much."

Relvis laughed and gave us a wave, tapping the horn to the tune of "Shave and a Haircut" as he drove away. We watched until the station wagon disappeared into the great, yawning sky.

"Relvis has left the building," Meredith said.

Then we both cracked up. We stood at the side of the Mojave Freeway, giggling, as the traffic rushed past us.

# 24

The next person who stopped for us was a transport truck driver named Zane. He was hauling water bottles and told us he had about a million bottles of water in the back of his truck. I don't know why anyone pays to drink water out of a plastic bottle when you can drink it out of the tap for free, but that's one of life's great mysteries. Zane wore a brown mesh Hooters hat and drank coffee out of a red Big Gulp mug. He had light-brown eyes and a five-o'clock shadow.

It was kind of squishy with all of us sitting up front, and Zane had to reach around my knee to work the stick-shift, so Meredith said she'd sit up in the back cab where Zane had a bed and a mini-fridge and a microwave and even a little TV with a Nintendo system hooked up to it.

"Sure, hop on back there," Zane said. "Don't mind the mess."

"This is cool," Meredith said, admiring the back cab.

"It ain't much, but it's what I got," Zane said. Zane was like a snail-turtle too and carried his house around behind him.

"Do you mind if I have a nap back here?" Meredith asked, lying down on the bed.

"Knock yourself out," Zane said.

Meredith zonked out right away, and Zane and I listened to talk-radio. After a while an announcer came on and said, "The verdict is in." And Zane turned the radio up loud. "The four LAPD officers accused of beating Rodney King last March have been acquitted," the announcer said.

"Fuck-damn," Zane whistled through his teeth. "That city's gonna burn." Then he rolled down his window and snot-rocketed onto the highway.

"We're going to L.A.," I said.

"Well, kid, you've got bigger balls than me."

I laughed.

"*Ooh, doggies!* Gonna see all hell break loose in the City of Angels tonight."

"Zane?"

"Yeah, kid?"

"What does *acquitted* mean?"

"Not guilty," Zane said.

"Oh," I said.

"You seen the video, though?"

I nodded. If it was the same video that had been on the news for a year, I knew the one he meant. It was a home-video of four white cops beating up a black guy real bad.

"So?" he said.

"So, what?" I said.

"So everyone's seen the video! So everyone knows those cops are guilty as charged!"

"Oh," I said.

"Think I'll head on over to my buddy's place in San Bernardino, lay low for a while. I suggest you do the same," he said.

"No way," I said. "We've got to get to Hollywood. Tonight."

Zane glanced back at Meredith. Then he looked at me hard for a moment. He sighed. "Well, I'll put a call out on the radio for you, see what I can do." Zane picked up the CB radio from its holder attached to the roof. "Breaker one-nine. This is Zane the Main Vein hauling the water train, headin' south on I-15, just comin' up to Baldy. Got an anklebiter and a YL with me, looking for a lift into Shaky Town. Can anyone nearby give them safe passage?"

There was only static over the radio for a long minute. Then a man's voice came on and said, "Ten-four, Veiner, this is Big Red," and he spoke in the same strange code as Zane had, but I figured out that he said he could give us a ride all the way into Los Angeles and that Zane should drop us at the Shell on Santa Fe Avenue and he'd collect us there.

"It worked!" I said, my heart ballooning inside my chest.

"Of course it worked," Zane said. "It's CB radio."

"That's the best thing ever."

"Yep," he said, nodding. "It pretty much is."

Then I put my hand up for Zane to give me high-five and he gave me a really good one and laughed and said, "You're all right, kid."

"Zane?" I said.

"Yeah?"

"How'd you learn to talk like that?"

Zane laughed. "Well, if you ever get to be a truck driver, you'll find out."

Then I thought that maybe trucking was something I *could* do when I grew up. I like to travel. I'm good at it, and I'd get to carry my house around behind me, plus, I'd get to learn a whole new secret language. I hated it when people asked me what I wanted to be when I grew up; I never knew what to say, so I always just told them the truth and said, "I don't know," but then they'd look so disappointed, like I'd done something wrong. Then they'd usually walk away because who wants to talk to a kid who doesn't even know what he wants to be when he grows up? So right that second I decided to start telling people that I wanted to be a trucker when I grew up. And it felt good.

Not too long after I'd decided to be a truck driver, Zane pulled into the Shell station, and we saw a guy with long dirty-blond hair wearing jeans and a white T-shirt leaning up against the front tire of a red dump truck, smoking a cigarette. He gave us a nod as Zane pulled his truck around. We all got out and the man walked over to us and Zane and the man shook hands. The man's name was Reginald but he said we could call him Reggie.

Meredith used the bathroom inside the Shell and I did too. I bought a Coke and a bag of dill pickle chips. Zane said to Reggie, "Watch out down there, my man, it's gonna be a mad, mad city tonight." And Reggie nodded like he wasn't too concerned one way or the other. We said goodbye and thanks to Zane and he said, "I hope you find what you're looking for in Hollywood." And I said, "Ten-four, Good Buddy," and he laughed and climbed into his rig and on the way out he pulled his air-horn and it was so loud that I wished I'd had time to plug my ears, but I was happy because Zane really was my good buddy, and now I had a pretty good idea of what I wanted to be when I grew up.

\*\*\*

Reggie drove an eighteen-wheeler tandem axel semi dump truck that carried twenty-seven tons of sand. We climbed up into the cab beside him and put our backpacks behind the front seat. He didn't play the radio or a tape and he had the CB volume turned so low you couldn't really hear what people were saying over it, but I didn't care because Reggie was nice and he was going to take us straight to Los Angeles without passing go or collecting 200 dollars. He answered all of my questions about his truck.

"I'd say the whole rig weighs about 80,000 pounds, all told," Reggie said.

"Whoa," I said. "That's like hauling an elephant!"

"That's like hauling five or six elephants." Reggie laughed.

"Whoa."

He smiled at me and handed me half of his sandwich.

I had a few bites and it was good but I could hardly eat because we were entering Los Angeles City Limits and I was so excited I thought

I'd pee my pants, even though I'd just peed at the Shell.

"I'm just going in to South Central to drop something off for my boss," Reggie said. "Then I'll show you where you can catch a bus over to Hollywood."

"Great!" I said.

"I can't believe it," Meredith said.

"Believe what?" I said.

"That we actually made it to L.A."

"Where are you two coming from?" Reggie asked.

"We're from Niagara Falls, but our car broke down near Albany, New York, so we've been hitching since then," Meredith said.

Reggie nodded. "Pretty big trek. Clear across the country. How many days it take you?"

"Five," I said, counting on my fingers.

"Hey, that's pretty good," Reggie said. "Couldn't have driven it much faster than that with only one driver," he nodded at Meredith.

"And we didn't even get kidnapped," I said, grinning.

"That's good," Reggie said. "No one wants that."

"Reggie?"

"Yeah, kid?"

"Do you like being a truck driver?"

He nodded. "Yeah, I'm pretty much living the dream," he said.

"The American Dream?"

Reggie laughed a little. "You could say that."

\*\*\*

The sky in Los Angeles was as blue as a swimming pool and the sun shone high and bright in the sky. Tall, tall palms lined the streets and stood so straight and proud, as if to welcome us, as if to say, *We're glad you made it*. There were thousands of glass buildings scraping up against the sky and more cars and people and stores and billboards than I could count. As we drove further into the centre of the city, the houses got smaller and so did the lawns. The cars got older and rustier too. Meredith asked Reggie if he had an extra smoke, and he said, "That shit'll kill ya," and Meredith said, "Not if something else does first." Then Reggie laughed and took one from his pack and handed it to her and they both smoked. I rolled my window down and let my arm hang out the side of the truck and the sun glinted off my side mirror so I couldn't see what was behind us anymore.

Then we were driving through this one neighbourhood and I thought, *People in Los Angeles are kind of weird*, because they were doing weird things like running into the middle of the road and yelling and throwing rocks at cars and waving bottles over their heads and flipping everyone the bird.

Then I started to get a bad feeling. A thick, heavy feeling way down in the bottom of my stomach. And I knew that something was wrong and something bad was going to happen, and there was nothing I could do to stop it.

Little white dots popped out all over Reggie's knuckles as he gripped the big steering wheel. "Something's up," he said. "Maybe get in the back."

So we climbed into the back cab. It wasn't set up all cozy like Zane's was. There was just a tool box, a hatchet, an old grey army blanket, a pile of candy wrappers, and a bunch of empty coffee cups back there. Reggie stopped at a red light and there was a *thunk* and a *craaaack* as a brick hit the windshield, and then another one, sending a million spider webs across the glass.

"Get down!" Reggie said.

"Oh, this is not good," Meredith said. "This is not healthy."

Then Reggie's door opened and a mad-looking black guy grabbed

Reggie and ripped him out of the truck. I crouched behind the driver's seat and could see a little bit through the space between the seat and the door. Meredith smushed herself up against me so that she could see too. Two men hurled what looked like a fire extinguisher at Reggie's head, and then the first guy hit him three times in the face with a claw hammer. "Oh my God," Meredith said as Reggie fell to his knees. She bit down on her knuckles. We watched through the crack in the door as four black guys took turns kicking Reggie. They kicked him in the head so hard, his head bounced off the pavement, again and again. I could hear him saying, "Stop, please, stop." But I knew that they wouldn't. One guy stepped on his neck while the others kicked him in the head. My hand closed around the hatchet. I could do something. I could chop their nuts off, I could save him. But those guys were so big and angry, they were men, and I was only a kid, and small for my age. Meredith put her backpack on and handed me mine and I put mine on. Then there was a noise so loud above us it sounded like the world was caving in, but I could feel the hard wind blowing through the door and realized it was a helicopter. Probably a police helicopter, I thought, come to save Reggie, to save us. But it didn't.

One of the guys took a huge slab of concrete, held it up high, then dropped it on Reggie's head. Then he danced a little jig over Reggie and pointed and laughed at him and gave the helicopter the finger. Meredith turned away from me and puked. Cherry-slush vomit flooded the back of the truck and soaked through my jeans. I didn't know what to do. I didn't know what to say. For a minute, I thought I was having a terrible dream. I slapped my cheeks and pinched my arms, but I couldn't wake up no matter how hard I tried, so I knew it must be real. A guy spat a big loogie on Reggie's face and then he and the guy who dropped the concrete on Reggie's head left. They just walked away, whooping and laughing and slapping each other high-fives. Where were the police? Where was the ambulance? I saw some people take out cameras and take pictures of Reggie lying there on the ground. Some people threw beer bottles at him and they exploded in bright brown bursts around his head. A man came up and rifled through Reggie's pockets and took his wallet, but no one did anything to help him. Not me, not Meredith, not anyone. Then we heard gunshots and the *ping* of bullets hitting the truck.

"We have to get out," Meredith said. "They're shooting at the truck."

I couldn't move. My legs were heavier than twenty-seven tons of sand.

"Come on, we have to go!" She pushed the door open, grabbed the hatchet, took my hand, and dragged me out of the cab. We ran across the intersection to a gas station and laid on our stomachs behind a sign for diesel. I felt dizzy and nauseous and sick. The whole world blurred around me.

"I can't see!" I said. "*I can't see!*"

Meredith put her hand inside the sleeve of her sweatshirt and wiped my eyes.

"Oh," I said.

"Shh."

"We have to get Reggie. We have to help him."

"We can't."

"But who's going to help him? Nobody's even *helping* him!"

"Look," she said. We watched as Reggie, head covered in blood, his white T-shirt stained red, struggled to get to all fours. He pushed his hand out in front of him again and again, like he was waving us away. His long hair fell in front of his face, streaked red with blood. He grabbed hold of the running board, staggered to his feet, and leaned against the open door of the cab for a few seconds. Then he started to crawl into his truck. A black lady ran to him and helped him get inside the truck. We could see Reggie's work-boots poking out the door as she laid him across the front seat. Then a black man and woman drove up in a little blue car. The man got out and the woman spun the car around so it pointed away from Reggie's truck, which was slowly creeping forward. Another big black guy ran up to the truck and hoisted himself into the driver's seat. The guy who came in the blue car stood outside on the running board, hanging onto the side mirror. The truck started and they drove away, pulling 80,000 pounds behind them.

"Do you think he's okay?" I said.

"No," Meredith said.

"This wasn't supposed to happen," I said. "It wasn't supposed to be like this."

"I know," she said.

"Was that our fault?"

"No. No way."

"We should have ... "

"We couldn't," she said.

"Do you think he'll die?"

"I don't know," Meredith said.

# 25

Hundreds of people ran by us screaming and yelling and smashing bottles in the street and throwing bricks and rocks at cars and shop windows. Cars full of men waved sticks and bats and guns as they drove past, shooting bullets up into the crystal blue sky. Tires squealed, cars crashed into each other, guys ran after cars and hit them with bats and sticks and rocks, reaching through the drivers' windows to take purses, wallets, cans of soda. Six guys picked up a white Buick and flipped it over and someone fired shots at the red news helicopter that hovered above the intersection.

"This ... this is ... " I had trouble getting my words out.

"This is a riot," Meredith said.

"Usually people say that when they're having fun."

"Not today," she said, her eyes scanning the intersection.

People ran around, smashing everything in sight, chanting, *"Rodney King! Rodney King!"* I knew who he was; he was the man on the video who was driving too fast and those cops had beat him up, and now, I guess, the cops weren't going to jail for it, and all of Los Angeles was going insane. People ran out of a liquor store across the street carrying bottles of wine, cases of beer, arm-loads of alcohol. Guys were shaking up beer bottles and spraying them over each other and laughing. They smashed the windows of the liquor store with steel bats and the glass crackled away. Someone set fire to a rag sticking out of a bottle and threw it into the liquor store and then the liquor store was on fire and we could see the smoke begin to build and flames licking around the edges of the broken window. You could hear the glass bottles that were still inside exploding in the heat. Then a white delivery truck stopped at the intersection and the same guys who had beat up Reggie surrounded the truck and one guy opened the door and pulled the driver out of his seat. They started beating on him, kicking him in the nuts, in the knees. He had brown hair and wore a grey T-shirt and jeans and he held his hands above his head, but they kept on kicking him until he fell. Once he was on the ground, they kicked him in the head over and over and over again. The same guy who had dropped the concrete slab on Reggie ripped the stereo system out of the truck and threw it at the driver's head. Another guy pulled out a Swiss Army knife and tried to cut the truck driver's ear off. He held up a little piece of flesh, dripping with blood, and waved it above his head like it was a trophy. I was shaking all over and the ground was wobbling and everything was wrong. A guy came up and took the truck driver's wallet out of his back pocket. Then he and the guys who had beat up Reggie started ripping the truck driver's clothes off. First his shirt, then his shoes and jeans and underwear, until he lay naked on the ground, covering his head with his arms. Another guy came up with a can of black spray paint and started spraying the truck driver's chest and his body and his privates black. People were laughing and pointing and taking pictures and some people ran up and kicked him and then ran back to their friends. It was the worst thing I'd ever seen and there was nothing I could do about it. I closed my eyes for a minute and told myself not to throw up. But it didn't work. I did throw up. A lot. Then Meredith was rubbing my back and saying, "It's okay, it's okay." And when I opened my eyes again someone was pouring a jerry can full of gasoline all over the truck driver and dumping it right into his face and mouth and eyes and people were still throwing bottles and rocks and trash at him and no one was doing anything to help him and someone in the crowd was videotaping the whole thing and I said, "It is *not fucking okay.*"

"You're right," Meredith said. "It's not."

Then a black man went over to the truck driver and you could tell he was a priest because he was wearing the black suit and the white collar that priests always wear, and the priest said, "Stop! Stop this!" but people still kept throwing rocks and bottles at the truck driver who lay unmoving on the pavement beside his truck while people took everything out of the back of his truck like furniture and instruments and stereos and whatever else he was hauling. Then the priest spread his arms wide and he held a book in one hand, probably a bible, and he hunkered down over the truck driver and covered him with his own body and yelled, "Kill him, and you'll have to kill me too!" Then the crowd booed and someone else threw a bottle that landed right beside the priest's head and a green shower exploded in his face, but the priest just shut his eyes and shook his head, and then across the street, someone threw a brick through the window of a convenience store, and you could hear the tinkle of glass and the sharp pops of gunshots a little further up the street.

I don't know if the priest did that because God told him to or if he did it because it was the right thing to do, maybe the *only* thing to do, but I was glad that there were people like that priest in the world, and I wished that I had been able to do that for Reggie.

Then people started flooding into the gas station and filling their cars and filling up jerry cans and bottles with gasoline. They were going into the store and taking whatever they wanted. People came out with bags full of chips and pop and cigarettes and magazines. One guy held a stack of lottery tickets in his teeth. A fat, pale man with light-brown hair stood across the street talking into a microphone and someone else was videotaping him, a blond guy. We watched as a group of people came at them and one guy took the microphone out of the news reporter's hand. "Hey," he said, "I'm a reporter." And the other guy started hitting him in the face and head with the microphone and yelling at him, "Get out of here! Get the fuck out of here! You don't belong here!" Then the cameraman dropped the video camera and took off running down the street and a bunch of people followed him, hurling rocks and bricks and bottles at him, and the reporter cowered, shielding his head and crying out until a big white van that read KTLA NEWS pulled up and opened its back door and the reporter hurled himself into the van and it sped away. A white Toyota Corolla drove through the intersection and someone threw a garbage can at it and it cracked the glass. The car stopped and some guys ran and pulled out the driver and it was a tall lady with red hair and she covered her face and screamed, "Don't hurt my baby! Don't hurt my baby!" and the crowd started whipping all kinds of things at her like beer cans and stones, and she got down on the ground and covered her head with her hands and a guy ran up and kicked her in the stomach and she rolled under her car so the guy opened the door of the car and a little kid crawled out, a little redheaded baby, it just plopped out onto the road and started crawling down the street, crying. Then a bus stopped on the corner and an Asian guy stepped off the bus and a mob of five or six people surrounded him and clobbered him, bashing in his face, punching him all over, and he tried to get back on the bus, but the bus closed its doors and drove on.

"What should we do?" I said.

Meredith pulled her hood up over her head and dug around in her backpack and pulled out a green bandana and tied it around her face so that only her eyes were showing. Then she took out a black toque and handed it to me. "Put this on," she said. "Pull it down low over your face."

"Why?"

"Because we're white."

I took out my knife and cut eye holes and a mouth hole in the toque so I could see and breathe. Meredith got to her feet. She took my hand and pulled me up, and together, we ran.

# 26

We didn't make it too far before someone threw a shopping cart at a car, the car spun out of control and slammed into the front window of a shoe store and a hundred people climbed over the hood of the car to load up on Adidas, Nikes, and Reeboks. Guys destroyed abandoned cars with tire irons and bats, and windshields lay in smithereens all over the road, bottle rockets sailed through the air, and car tires screeched like cats in the night. I could hear gunshots and glass smashing all around me and then Meredith was pulling me inside a little hot dog stand that was painted blue and white and said ART'S CHILI DOGS. There was no one inside, but all the food and drinks were there. Meredith closed the door and locked it and we sat on the floor. She pulled her bandana down, and I took off my toque.

"Are you hungry?" Meredith said.

"I don't know," I said.

"Thirsty?" she handed me a cream soda from the cooler beside us and took a Coke for herself. "I don't know when we'll be able to eat or drink again."

We could hear the crowd rage on outside. I drank the cream soda and tried to think. "I don't know what to do," I said.

"We have to get out of here," she said. "We could die."

"What about finding my father?"

"If he *is* here, he's probably trying to get out too."

I looked down at my hands. They were shaking. I had come all this way, I had done all the right things, and I *still* didn't get to meet him. It wasn't fair. There's nothing fair about life. Not one single thing. You just have to get through it the best way you know how.

I put my head in my hands. We could hear people outside

screaming, *"No Justice, No Peace!"* over and over and over again. "No Justice, No Peace!" Then we heard a big *whoosh* and a *POW!* and we both lay flat on the floor and covered our heads.

"What was that?" I whispered.

"Probably a car exploding," Meredith whispered.

"Meredith?"

"Yeah?"

"I'm scared."

"Me too," she said.

Then we slowly sat up again and she skooched closer to me and gave me a hug. "Oh," she said, looking at my pants.

"What?" I looked down. There was a big wet spot, like I had peed. It smelled like pee. But I didn't remember peeing. Or thinking that I had to go. But there it was, darkening my jeans, running down my leg. "I can't believe it."

"Don't worry about it," Meredith said. "It doesn't matter."

And as completely humiliating and totally awful as it was that I had peed my pants, she was right. At that moment, it didn't really matter that much. I pressed my eye up to a crack in the door. "There's a payphone right outside," I said. "We could call Gina."

"Gina's in Niagara Falls," Meredith said. "She can't help us."

She was right, of course, but I still wanted to talk to Gina at that moment more than anyone had ever wanted to talk to another person in the history of the world.

Then someone threw a brick through the window of Art's Chili Dogs and glass shattered all over us.

"Fuck!" Meredith said, shaking out her hoodie.

A guy peered through the busted-out window and saw us and turned his head and yelled to someone else, "Hey, there's white people in here! Get over here! We'll get 'em," and he started climbing through the window. We stood up, then the guy's friend ran up and looked at us and said, "Those are just kids, man, *shit*." And the other guy said, "Who cares?" and started coming for us. I opened the door and pulled the toque over my face and Meredith put her bandana back on and she held the hatchet up high and we ran. We ran and ran and ran and ran and ran.

Everywhere I looked, people were doing the wrong thing. People threw bricks through the windows of stores and cars, and people pushed and shoved and trampled over each other to get inside and take whatever they could. I saw someone drive a Jeep through the front doors of a furniture store and people come out carrying couches, mattresses, and bedside tables. I saw two men knock sledgehammers through the windows of a Radio Shack and people load TVs, ghetto blasters, VCRs, video cameras, and computers into shopping carts and the backs of trucks and cars and haul them away. I saw a bunch of kids pour out of a party supplies store. They carried a unicorn piñata and threw sparkly confetti all over each other. I saw a man wrecking a red Volkswagen Beetle with a golf club. I saw a lady pushing a piano down the street. I saw a brown UPS van turned on its side, burning in a parking lot. I saw people coming out of a grocery store with chips and cereal and melons and so many diapers. I saw three little kids roll burning tires down the street. I saw Asian men with shotguns up on the roofs of their stores, shooting at people who tried to break in. I saw a man set fire to a bus bench. I saw two little boys run out of a costume shop wearing rainbow-coloured clown wigs. I saw four teenagers stagger under the weight of a refrigerator. I saw a woman pulling a rack of clothes from the drycleaners down the sidewalk. I saw three guys rip an ATM out of a wall. I saw four white nuns in a black Cadillac speeding down the street. I hoped they were praying in there, praying for all of us. A black man stood outside of his tobacco shop, screaming at the crowd. "Why are you doing this? Why do you gotta wreck *my* store?" he yelled at the top of his lungs.

"I'm *with* you! I'm from the ghetto *too*. I tried to *make* it! I tried to *give* you something, give you a store. It's not *right!* It's not *right* what you're doing! I'm like *you!* I'm not *the man!* Why you have to steal *my* computer? Wreck *my* store? I tried to make it." His voice was cracking and tears sparkled down his cheeks. We kept running. Waterfalls of glass crashed over us as we passed a thousand angry faces. We tripped over splintered husks of plywood. The air was thick and oily. Chunks of ash and embers fell all around us. Everywhere I looked, buildings and cars and tires burned, sending black pillars of smoke up into the clear blue sky.

"Stop," I said, tugging Meredith backwards by her shirt.

Her hair flew crazily around her head from the wind of the chopper blades above us. "What?" she said.

"I can't run anymore. My throat ... I can't breathe."

"Come on." She pulled me into the doorway of a barber shop and we leaned against the plywood that was boarding it up. Someone had spray-painted it, BLACK OWNED in huge black letters. White piles of broken glass lined the street. There were steps in front of the barber shop and we sat down on them to rest for a minute.

"Oh, shit," Meredith said.

I looked down at her lap. A dark puddle spread across it and leaked out onto the steps.

"You peed too," I said, half-laughing.

"That's not pee," she said.

"Oh," I said. "*Shit.*"

She grabbed my arm. "We have to get somewhere safe. Inside. Right now."

# 21

We went inside the shop next door which had a red and blue sign out front that read KOREAN GROCERY. Noodles and packages of crackers were scattered everywhere. Glass jars of stringy red stuff lay broken in the aisles. Huge sacks of rice lay split open in front of us, spilling their guts out onto the floor. A chubby black teenage girl stood in the first aisle holding a wire basket. She picked a package of noodles off a shelf, turned it over, then politely put it back. A Korean man stood behind the counter and pointed a shotgun at us.

"Get out," he said. "We no want you here."

We put our hands above our heads. Meredith dropped the hatchet and it clattered to the floor.

"She's having a baby," I said, pointing at Meredith.

Meredith held her belly and moaned. Then a Korean woman popped up from behind the counter. Her black hair was glossy and fell to her shoulders. She wore a cream-coloured blouse. From the way she looked at Meredith, I knew she would help us. She looked at the man and said something to him in Korean. Then he said something to her that I didn't understand but sounded kind of harsh. Then she yelled at him. Then he lowered the shotgun and shrugged his shoulders, and she stepped out from behind the counter and came toward us.

"Come, come," she said, motioning for us to follow her to the back of the store.

We followed her to a door that read EMPLOYEES ONLY. She opened the door and led us into a tiny back room. There was a yellow bucket and a dirty mop dripping into a drain in the floor. Shelves filled with cleaning supplies and other junk lined the walls. Beside the door was a desk covered in ashtrays, receipts, spiral notebooks, calculators, and Jolly Rancher wrappers. There was a computer on the desk, and even though it was turned off, it seemed to be staring at us with its square, unblinking eye. A short, grey sofa was pressed up against the side wall and the woman took down a blue and white checkered tablecloth from a shelf above the desk. The plastic crinkled as she unfurled it and spread it over the sofa. Then she motioned for Meredith to lie down.

Meredith turned away from us and slid her pants off. She took a grey hoodie from her backpack and used it to cover herself. She sat sideways on the sofa and leaned her back against the arm, putting her legs into a diamond shape in front of her. Her face was squeezed up tight like a fist.

"Oh, *God*," she said. "This wasn't supposed to happen."

"Are you having a boy or a girl?" the woman asked.

"I don't know," Meredith said.

"I have three boys," the woman said. "All born in America. Oldest one seventeen now," she smiled. Her teeth were white and square as Chiclets. She took a green plastic bowl and a white rag down from the shelf. She filled the bowl with cold water and soaked the rag in it. She wrung out the rag and folded it into a rectangle and carefully placed it on Meredith's forehead. Meredith's face became smooth again.

"Thank you," Meredith said, reaching out her hand.

The Korean woman took Meredith's hand in her own and squeezed it. "You're welcome," she said. "My husband call 9-1-1 for you," she said.

"They won't come," Meredith said. "There's too much," she waved her hand toward the door.

"They'll come," the woman said. "They don't give up on people in America."

Meredith moaned. I watched as thick red ribbons of blood snaked across the tablecloth. I looked at the woman and her dark eyes flashed with something I couldn't know.

"They'll come," the woman said. Then she filled a white plastic kettle with water and plugged it into the wall. I wondered who could want a cup of tea at a time like this.

Meredith cried out again and another gush of blood slid around the tablecloth. Her face was as pale as the moon. She dug her nails into the tablecloth and screamed. More and more blood came, but still no baby.

The Korean woman left the room for a few minutes and while she was gone, I went into the far corner and took my pee-stained jeans and underwear off and changed into new undies and my Adidas trackpants. I wadded up my jeans and underoos and stuffed them into the garbage bin beside the desk. I knew Gina would be mad because they were my expensive Bugle Boy jeans, but I knew I wouldn't be able to find a laundromat anywhere, and plus, I didn't even know if pee ever washed out of clothes. Sometimes, throwing things away is the best thing you can do with them.

I pulled a chair over and sat beside Meredith. I made sure the cloth on her head stayed wet and that she had whatever she asked for. She never asked for anything, so I wasn't really much use. Except for once, she asked for her mom. And I couldn't do anything about that, either.

After about two hours, Meredith was surrounded in a pool of her own blood. It dripped onto the floor and crept toward the drain. I closed my eyes and saw Brian, bleeding on the floor of the TV room at Bright Light, losing everything. Meredith jerked and screamed and kicked her legs. She needed help, anyone could see that. The Korean woman sat on the edge of the desk. She drank a can of iced tea and looked worried.

"I'll be right back," I said, then I left the little room and ran out the back door to find someone. A nurse, a doctor, a veterinarian, anyone. The air was smoky and garbage littered the streets. The sun was gone and the sky looked bruised and hollow. There were only angry people around, no cops, no ambulance, no doctors. I climbed the fire escape to the roof of the store so I could get a better look. Maybe I could see the hospital and somehow get her there. Maybe I could signal to a helicopter to come get us, or send help. I stood on top of the roof and looked out over the city of Los Angeles.

Everywhere, everywhere, fires burned.

In the distance, I saw a red fire engine and fire fighters spraying water at a huge building that must have been a shopping mall. It was hard to believe my eyes, but people were actually *attacking* the fire fighters while they worked. Launching rocks and bottles at them and jumping onto their backs as they hosed down the blaze. "HELP!" I screamed out over the city. "*HELP US!*"

I screamed until I lost my voice. I took off my sweater and waved it over my head in the shape of S.O.S. so that the news helicopter would see me and send help. It paused for a second, the propeller driving dust and ash into my eyes, then it took a hard right and buzzed away. I don't know if it saw me, I didn't know if it would do anything, but it was all I had.

I was eleven years old. I didn't know anything. But I knew enough to see that this was probably the end of the world.

\*\*\*

When I got back to the room, the pool of blood around Meredith was even bigger, and she was clutching a bundle of rags to her chest. But then the bundle of rags made a mewling sound like a kitten, and I realized what it was.

"You had a baby," I said.

Meredith looked up at me, her green eyes shining with tears. "A girl," she said.

"Wow."

She tilted the bundle a little so I could see it. The baby was red-dish-purple, and her face looked like a raisin.

"Wow," I said again.

"Tucker," Meredith grabbed my shirt. "If I don't make it, you have to look after her."

"You're going to make it," I said. I looked down at my shoes. They were covered in blood.

"But if I don't," she said.

I looked at Meredith. She was a whiter shade of pale.

The Korean woman stood at the desk, holding a phone to her ear. I could hear the busy signal. She hung up and redialled, again and again.

"Take good care of her, Tucker. Teach her everything you know."

"But I don't know anything!"

"You do. You're good."

I shook my head.

"Teach her how to be a good person."

I swallowed and snot strings reached to the floor and I realized I was crying. "What's her name?" I asked, wiping my face.

Meredith closed her eyes for a moment. "I was thinking ... Relvis."

I stared at her.

Her lips cracked as her face broke into a smile. "Just kidding," she said.

I laughed a tiny little laugh.

"What do you think of Angel?"

"She's born in City of Angels," the Korean woman said, nodding. She handed Meredith a glass of water.

"It's nice," I said and thought of Gina.

Meredith thanked the lady and sipped the water, then closed her eyes for a while. The baby's eyes were grey like the ocean before a storm. She had a downy patch of black hair and see-through fingernails. She was smaller than the rabbit we had buried in Arizona, which seemed like a gazillion years ago, but was only the day before. She nuzzled into Meredith's breast, and I felt like I shouldn't watch, but I couldn't look away.

Then there was a smashing sound from the front of the store and we could hear people yelling. The Korean woman left the room, closing the door behind her with a click.

"When you get home, take her to see Steve," Meredith mumbled. "My brother. He'll know what to do."

"Meredith, you're going to be okay. Everything's going to be okay."

"All shall be well," she said quietly. "And all shall be well, and all manner of things shall be well." She closed her eyes.

"That's right," I said.

Then we heard a blast of gunshots from the front of the store. *BANG. BANG. BANG. BANG.*

Meredith shuddered. "Come here," she whispered, looking at me with her beach-glass eyes.

I leaned my face in close to hers. She turned her head and kissed me softly on the cheek. The moment lasted a sweet forever. Then, she was gone.

# 28

I couldn't remember what anything meant.

There was a riot outside.

My best friend was dead.

There was a tiny newborn baby wrapped in rags and J-cloths.

I had to get the heck out of Dodge.

*\*\**

I took everything out of Meredith's backpack and made a nest for the baby inside it with the softest T-shirts she had. Then I wrapped the baby in my extra sweater so she would stay warm, and I put her inside the backpack and left the zipper open a bit so she could breathe. I got my plastic bag of special stuff out of my backpack, untied the knot, and took out Charlie, my little dog. I gave him a pat on the head and put him in Meredith's palm and closed her hand around him. I left Charlie with Meredith because he was the best thing I had. And because then, I knew that when I left, she wouldn't be alone.

I put Meredith's stuff in my backpack and put it on my back and strapped the baby-backpack to my front, and walked out of the room.

I didn't see anyone in the store.

I didn't see the Korean man lying behind the counter with a bullet in his forehead.

I didn't see his wife, who had helped us the best she could, bleeding from the stomach behind the magazine rack.

I didn't see the young black guy seizing on the floor of the candy aisle with his hand over his heart.

And I didn't see the dark-haired guy, lying face down beside the cooler with a hole the size of an egg in the back of his head.

I didn't see any of that. I just walked through the store and out onto the sidewalk and into the angry L.A. night.

# 29

I walked and walked and walked and walked. When I got tired, I kept walking. When I got thirsty, I kept walking. When I got scared, I kept walking. Everywhere people were looting and breaking things, setting fire to whatever they could. Lots of people wore T-shirts and shorts, but I was cold, and I shivered as I walked. A thin, white layer of ash covered everything, and everything was so loud. All of the noises put together made the worst sound. People screaming and smashing things, the crackle of fires, the crunch of buildings collapsing as they burned, the crash of glass as it shattered, the pop-pop of gunshots, and the *ca-thunk* of cars as they were flipped over. It was the sound of a city tearing itself apart.

The baby, Angel, started to cry, so the next time I passed a grocery store, I went in and took some stuff. I knew it was wrong, but there was no other way to get it since no one was working. I went to the baby aisle and took a bottle, four cans of formula, and I looked and looked for diapers, but all of the shelves where the diapers should've been were empty, so I took a roll of paper towels instead. I went to the check-out counter and took the baby out of Meredith's backpack and put her down on the conveyor belt. I unwrapped the J-cloth from around her butt and put it in the garbage can behind the till. When I saw the purply stub of her umbilical cord, I got dizzy, because I knew that only a few hours before, that same cord had been connected to Meredith. The Korean woman had tied a green piece of string around it, and the knots were so tight, they could never be undone. I unwound a big roll of paper towels and wrapped them around her in the shape of a diaper. I took a bottle of water out of the cooler beside the till and then I opened the can of formula with the can-opener on my Swiss Army knife. I poured some formula into the baby bottle and mixed it with water like the directions on the side of the can said to do. I took a pencil from a cup of pens and pencils that sat on the drawer of the till and stirred it up with the pencil. Then I picked up the baby and held her in my arms the way I had seen mothers do. I tried to get her to drink from the bottle. At first she turned her head away and spat and gurgled and cried a bit. But after a while she let me put the bottle in her mouth and she sucked on it and took some formula. People were coming in and out of the store, loading up carts and bags with cereal, ice cream, cheese, pepperoni sticks, whatever was left. Nobody noticed me and the newborn baby. I wrapped her up in my sweater again and put her back inside the backpack and nestled her in there so she was warm and comfortable. On my way out, I grabbed a Coke and a Kit Kat and put them in my backpack for later.

***

I was on a main road and a bunch of cars passed me, and I thought about sticking my thumb out and asking for a ride, but I didn't really want to ride in any of those cars. What I *really* wanted was a ride in Doc Brown's DeLorean. Then I could go back in time to before, when Meredith was alive and everything was okay in the world. We never would have come to L.A. We never would have left Niagara Falls. I would still have a best friend, and her baby would still have a mother.

I realized that it was my fault that Meredith was dead, and a wall of glass broke inside my chest. My throat lumped up, and the edges of everything got blurry.

Then a black man in a white Ford Bronco cruised up beside me and rolled down his window. "Where're ya headed, kid?"

"I don't know," I said, wiping my eyes.

"I'm going to the airport, if you want a ride," he said.

"I don't know," I said.

"Well, tell you what *I* know," he said. "Sometimes, you gotta get the hell out of L.A. This is one of those times."

I nodded.

Then the man gave me a little wave and took off. I watched the white Bronco as it headed down the road; it seemed to be going in slow motion. But everything was going in slow motion, so I couldn't be absolutely 100-percent sure about anything.

I walked for a long, long time and didn't think about anything except that I was leaving Los Angeles. I walked toward the bright lights of the planes I could see coming in to land somewhere in the distance. I passed a woman with grey hair leaning in the doorway of a camera store.

"Hey!" she called out to me.

"Hey," I said.

"Do you know what's going on?" Her face was pinched and tired, and her eyes looked like someone had knocked the light out of them.

"Not really," I said. "There's a riot." I shrugged and felt the baby jostle against my stomach.

"It's those pigs, I'll bet. The police in this city are goddamned animals." She spat onto the sidewalk.

"Do you know which way the airport is?"

"Sure, yeah," she said. Her head twitched twice to the side. "Just stay on this street for quite a ways, then you'll want to take a right onto Century Boulevard. Then you just keep going straight until you get on a plane."

"Thanks," I said.

"Got any change?"

I gave her what I had in my pocket, a couple of ones and a few quarters.

"May God bless you," she said.

"Thanks," I said, and kept walking.

\*\*\*

When I got to the airport, the first thing I did was use the washroom. I hung the baby-backpack on the hook on the back of the door and Angel didn't cry or fall out or anything. The second thing I did was call Gina. There was no answer in her room but I let it ring about a thousand times anyways. Then I hung up. Then I went looking for money. I carefully took Angel out of Meredith's backpack so I could have a good look through it. She stayed wrapped inside her sweater-nest on a chair beside me and didn't even cry. I found $200 safety-pinned inside a secret pocket in the top flap of Meredith's backpack, plus another $187 in her wallet. And I still had a $130 of my own. I thought that would be enough to buy a plane ticket to Buffalo, and then I could hitchhike the rest of the way back to Niagara Falls. I took off Angel's paper-towel diaper and wrapped a new one around her, then folded the sweater around her again to keep her warm. I zipped Angel back inside the backpack leaving only a little air hole open and went up to the ticketing counter.

"That flight doesn't leave until five a.m. tomorrow," the man behind the counter said. He was blond and fat and had crumbs stuck in his moustache.

"Okay," I said. "I'll take it."

"It's sold out," he said.

"Oh."

"The next flight to Buffalo is at eleven-fifty a.m. and it is ... " he checked his computer, "also fully booked."

"What about Toronto?" I said.

"Canada?" he said.

I nodded.

He clicked some buttons on the keyboard. "The next flight to Toronto leaves at seven thirty-five a.m. Unfortunately, it is fully booked as well. Over-sold, actually." He gave me a thin smile.

"I just need to get home," I said.

"I can put you on stand-by," he said.

"What's that?"

"If someone doesn't show up for their flight, you'll get their seat."

"What if everybody shows up?"

"Then ... you don't get a seat," he said.

"Oh," I said. "Can I stand up on the plane?"

"No," he said.

"Oh," I looked down at my shoes. I didn't like looking at my shoes though, because they were stained with Meredith's blood. So I looked back up at him and his stupid, crumby moustache.

"How old are you?" he said.

"Eleven."

"And you're flying alone today?"

"Yes."

"Do you have a letter of authorization from your parent or guardian?"

"No."

"I'm afraid we'll need to see some sort of documentation before—"

"Look, my mom is in the hospital in Niagara Falls. My best friend just died in the back of a Korean grocery store. I don't know where my father is, and Los Angeles is on fire. I need to go home *now*."

He looked at me for a few seconds then pressed his lips together. "I see," he said. He looked at his computer screen and clicked some buttons. Then he sighed. "Well, we can just keep trying to get you on stand-by for the next available flight to Buffalo or Toronto."

"Thank you," I said.

"I can't guarantee that you'll get a seat though."

"So, I'll just have to wait and see?"

"That's right," he said, eyeing the TV screen that hung from the ceiling, showing the zillions of fires burning across L.A.

"I just want to go home," I said.

He nodded and checked me through. "You can pay at the gate if you get a seat," he said.

When I went through security, I put the baby-backpack on the conveyor belt, and Angel zipped right through the X-ray machine. Nobody said anything about her. Maybe they thought she was a doll. Maybe the person who was supposed to be looking at the X-ray machine was actually watching the TV that hung across the room. Everyone in the airport kept watching the TVs, then looking at each other and shaking their heads.

I found a quiet corner near my departure gate and leaned against the wall and drank my Coke and ate my Kit Kat. Then I took Angel out of the backpack and gave her some more formula. She gurgled and it gooped down her chin in little white rivers. I wiped her off with a paper towel and tried again until she drank some of it. Then I wrapped her in my hoodie and put her back in the backpack and lay down so that I could see her. She looked at me with her big grey ocean eyes.

"I'm sorry," I whispered.

She blinked at me a few times and screeched a little bit, but she didn't cry. After a while she closed her eyes, and so did I. The tears came hot and fast, and I was glad for it.

\*\*\*

Everyone showed up for the five a.m. flight to Buffalo. Everyone showed up for the seven thirty-five a.m. flight to Toronto, plus some extra people who couldn't get on and were upset about it. Everyone showed up for the eleven-fifty a.m. flight to Buffalo. Everyone showed up for the afternoon flight to Toronto. But I kept trying. I went back and forth between the two departure gates all day. It was a long way to go because one was in the International terminal and one was Domestic. Sometimes I had to run between the two to get there on time. But all of the people with tickets showed up for their flights. I guess everyone thought it was a good time to get the heck out of L.A., just like the guy in the Bronco said. I even asked a few nice-looking people if they would sell me their seats. One guy said he would, except that his mom had just died and he had to go to her funeral. One lady said she would, but her apartment was burned down in the riot and she had no place to stay so she was going to stay with her cousin in Buffalo. One guy just looked at me and said, "Not hardly, pal."

I didn't eat anything because I was afraid if I spent my money on food I wouldn't have enough left for the plane ticket. I just drank water and kept feeding formula to Angel every couple of hours. Angel was really good and didn't cry or fuss at all, she just slept and slept, but I was afraid to go to sleep again in case I missed a flight I could get on. I made sure her paper towel was always dry and that she stayed warm in her little nest. The backpack started to smell like cottage cheese, but she looked happy enough. I tried calling Gina a few more times but there was still no answer. I watched the live news footage of the riots that played on the TVs and saw that it was still going on and getting worse, and when I remembered the things I had seen people doing, I wanted to upchuck all over LAX.

Most people in the airport seemed pretty worried and upset too. Some people cried and were comforted by others, some people cried alone.

The sunset was a purple haze. I leaned my head against a glass wall and watched the sun drop toward the ocean like a big red Plinko chip. I waited at gate number forty-seven for the last flight to Buffalo, crossing my fingers on both hands. And my toes. The redheaded airport lady at the gate knew I was trying to get on the plane because I'd been trying to get on it for over twelve hours. I looked away from the window and watched her as she checked her computer and spoke into a walkie-talkie. Then she looked at me and did that thing with her finger that people do when they want you to come over to them.

I ran over to her.

"You still want to get on this flight?" she said.

"*Yes!*"

"You're lucky, someone hasn't shown up."

I hugged her and she laughed. "Thank you," I said.

"Get home safe, kiddo," she said.

Then I ran over to the window where I'd left Angel in her backpack and strapped the backpack to my chest and paid the money for the ticket and got on the plane.

# 30

As the flight attendants explained how to put on an oxygen mask, I thought of Meredith. Well, Meredith's body, stuck in the back of the Korean Grocery store. What would happen to her, and who would make sure she had a proper funeral and a proper burial, and who would plant a red fern beside her gravestone? Would she even get a gravestone? I didn't know the answers to anything, and I didn't know what I could do about any of it. I watched the pretty flight attendant show us how to click two parts of the seatbelt together and tried not to think about anything.

I sat between a lady and an old man. The lady got the window seat. She had ginormous breasts and a glass eye. She told me that her name was Linda and she had flown to L.A. to audition for a part in a movie about a weatherman who wakes up and it's the same day, over and over again.

"Sounds like kind of a boring movie," I said. "No offense."

She shrugged. "I think it'll probably be one of those movies that people either really love or really hate. If it ever gets made, that is."

"What part would you play? If you get it, I mean."

"The love interest," she nodded and her glass eye bobbed up and down.

"Do you think you got it?"

"The audition was cancelled!" she said. "Because of the riots. All of Hollywood's shut down, if you can believe it." She blew her nose into a Kleenex. "I'm just glad I made it out of there before the airport closed," she said. "Did you know we just got on one of the last flights out of L.A.?"

"No."

"They're shutting it down. Who knows for how long."

"The whole airport?"

"That's right. And the buses too."

"To everywhere?"

"No one comes in, no one leaves. Not until they get a handle on this thing."

"How are they going to do that?"

"What? Get a handle on it?"

"Yeah."

"They've had to call in the National Guard," she said.

"The army?"

"If you can believe it."

Then Angel coughed and spit up a gob of milky white stuff. The old man beside me chuckled and snorted a bit.

"Is that one of those dolls that wets itself and cries and everything?" Linda said.

"Not exactly," I said.

"It looks so real," Linda said, peering into the backpack. "My niece works in a doll factory in New Jersey. They're making them so life-like now, it's amazing."

The man sitting on my other side said, "That's no doll, lady. That's the real thing."

Linda looked at me. I nodded. She looked at Angel again. Then back to me. "Just what exactly are you doing with a baby in your backpack, young man?"

"It's kind of a long story," I said. "Would you mind if I just looked out the window for a while?"

Linda looked at me for a moment and her real eye got sad and her glass one kind of floated to the side as she nodded. "Sure, sure. That's fine. You can tell me about it some other time." Then she turned to look out the window, and I leaned forward so I could see out the window too.

The trees were green and the land was brown and the ocean was shimmery blue, sparkling in the day's last light. You would never know that things were such a giant mess in the world from 30,000 feet in the air.

After a while, I fed Angel some formula and then she fell asleep and so did Linda. Linda snored as she slept but her glass eye didn't close. It rolled around to the side and stared straight at me. The eye was milky-blue and it gave me the heebie-jeebies. I wanted to reach up and pull her eyelid shut over it, but I didn't. Instead, I stared at the grey seat-back in front of me and wished that Meredith was there.

The man in the aisle seat next to me said, "That your baby?"

"It's my best friend's baby," I said. "She died yesterday."

The man nodded slowly. "You gonna look out for her now, then?"

I looked down at Angel, curled up like a bean, sleeping. I nodded.

"That's good. That's good," he said, nodding. Then the man reached into his bag and slid out a yellow pamphlet and put it in my lap. "Have you accepted Jesus into your heart, son?"

I looked at the pamphlet then looked at him. "I'm not your son," I said.

He stared at me for a second. "Would you like to say the Sinner's Prayer with me?" he said.

"What's that?" I said.

"It's when you invite Jesus into your heart."

"Jesus can come into my heart if he wants to, I guess," I said. "There's other people in there too, so I guess one more can't hurt."

The man looked at me and I looked at him. His face was wrinkled like an old paper bag.

"Okay, then," he said and bowed his head. He began to pray. I think he wanted me to repeat after him, but I didn't. I just listened to him. He went on for quite a while and before he was finished, I fell asleep.

***

When I got off the plane in Buffalo, I could tell by the cool, fresh air and the quiet shush of traffic that things were okay in the state of New York, and people weren't rioting or killing each other or wrecking their own city. The sun was rising and hot-pink light shot through the clouds. I walked away from the airport and kept my thumb out and pretty soon a car picked me up. It was a gold Nissan 240SX. A man with icy-blue eyes drove and he told me his name was Paul. His girlfriend was Karla and she sat in the passenger seat and had puffy blonde hair. I asked them where they were headed and they said St. Catherines and they said they could take me to Niagara Falls, no problem, since they had to go through there anyways to get home.

They asked me all kinds of questions about where I was from and where I was going and they especially wanted to know all about Angel and where her mother was. But I didn't want to talk about Meredith with them so I just said, "She died in Los Angeles yesterday." And they said they were sorry to hear that. Angel woke up and started squirming and making small squeaky noises. Karla turned around and cooed at her and made mushy faces at her. She asked if she could hold her. But Karla had long fake nails that were painted salmon-colour and looked sharp, and I didn't want her to scratch Angel's skin with them. I told her that Angel was just born the day before and she was premature so she probably shouldn't be held by too many people or else she could get sick, which was probably true.

"Oh," Karla said, scrunching up her face. "Okay then." She looked at Paul with a pouty mouth and Paul glanced back at us, then back at her and shrugged.

Other than her salmon nails, Karla looked pretty normal and so did Paul. But there was something about them that made me feel cold and shivery inside. It was a watery, heavy feeling in my guts. I remembered how Meredith had said that sometimes the most normal looking people can be the weirdest people, and I figured that was probably true about Karla and Paul. We didn't say too much for the rest of the ride. As we were going across the Rainbow Bridge, it started to rain really hard. It seemed to me like the sky was crying.

We pulled up to the border crossing and Paul talked to the guard. The guard was a freckle-faced guy with big teeth. Paul told him they were returning from a trip to see their friends in Buffalo.

"This your son?" the guard said, nodding at me.

"My nephew."

I nodded at the guard.

He nodded to me again.

I thought that it was kind of strange at first that Paul lied to him about me being his nephew, but then I remembered the signs that I had seen in some places that said, *It is illegal to pick up hitchhikers,* so I figured that's why he lied. So he wouldn't get in trouble.

Paul talked to the guard a bit longer and then the guard said, "Have a nice day," and waved us through.

I stared at the falls and rolled down my window so I could hear them thunder as we drove past.

"Where should I drop you off, kid?" Paul asked.

"At the hospital, please."

"Sure thing," he said.

"Ew," Karla said. "I hate hospitals."

"Better than morgues," Paul said. Then they laughed.

As we pulled in front of Niagara General I thanked them and got out of the car carefully so I wouldn't hit the baby-backpack against anything.

"Maybe see you around, then," Karla said.

"Yeah," I said. But even though they were nice enough and gave me a ride and everything, I hoped that I would never see them again for as long as I lived. I felt a feeling when I was in the car with them, and it was not good. It was not good at all.

# PART THREE

# HOME IS WHERE YOUR MOM IS

# 31

I made sure Angel was all right in her backpack and she was sound asleep, so I strapped the backpack to my chest and went inside the hospital and took the elevator up to Gina's floor. Heather stood behind the desk eating a muffin as I came down the hall. I zipped the backpack all the way up so that Heather wouldn't get upset about Angel being in there and try to take her away from me. She looked at me and smiled and set down her muffin. When I got up to the desk she said, "She's been discharged."

"What?"

"Sent home. Two or three days ago now."

"Oh," I said. "So ... she's all better?"

"She's in recovery."

"Oh."

"Wait," Heather said. "I've got something for you, hold on a sec." She went into the little room behind the nurse's counter and came back with a honey-dip donut and handed it to me.

"Thanks," I said. "Did she leave a message for me or anything?"

"Nope, not that I know of."

"Okay. Thanks, Heather." I walked as fast as I could back to the elevator without jostling Angel around too much.

"Good to see you, Tucker!" Heather called down the hallway.

I waved to her as the elevator doors closed and she waved back. I ate the donut on the way down to the main floor and wondered what the world would be like if everyone was as nice as Heather.

I didn't know exactly where to find Gina but I started walking toward the Niagara Motel. The rain made the smoky smell of the fires come out of my hair; it smelled like something else too, something hard and mean. Angel was zonked out and I zipped the backpack almost all the way up, leaving only a tiny air-hole so she wouldn't get wet.

When I got to the Niagara Motel, Chad was behind the desk. I watched him as he cracked an egg into a glass of beer and drank it. Then he burped and lit a cigarette. "Holy shit," he said when he finally looked up and saw me. "I thought you were dead."

"Not yet," I said.

"Where's my fucking car?" he said.

"It's on the side of the highway near Albany, New York. Or, at least, that's where it was last Friday." I took off my backpack and fished around in it for a minute.

"It broke down?"

"Yep."

"Son of a slut!" he banged the edge of his fist into the counter.

"Here," I said. "I rescued this for you." I handed him the baby-blue lace garter belt.

He looked at it and blinked.

"It was on your sun visor," I said.

"Yeah, I know," he said.

"I thought you might want it."

"What I *want* is my car," he said, stuffing the garter belt into his pocket. "Where's Meredith?"

"Meredith died yesterday in Los Angeles, California," I said.

"Get the fuck out of here," he said.

"But ... I don't know where else to go."

"She's dead?"

I nodded.

"How?"

I unzipped the baby-backpack and showed him the contents.

"Holy shit," he said, pressing his palm to his forehead.

"Is Gina here?"

"Huh?"

"Gina? Gina Malone? My mom?"

"Room one-oh-eight," he said and handed me the key as he stared at Angel.

"Thanks," I said. I started to walk down the hallway but turned around halfway. "Chad?"

"Yeah?"

"I'm sorry about your car," I said.

He shrugged. "I can get another one."

I nodded and turned around and kept walking until I got to room one-oh-eight.

***

I tried the knob and it wasn't locked so I went in. Gina sat on the bed reading a magazine and eating Doritos. "Tucker!" She opened her arms and I ran to her. I let her hold me and kiss me all over and cry and cry and I cried too and then the baby woke up and she started to cry too.

I told Gina everything, well, all of the important parts. I left out some stuff that she didn't need to know about, like me shooting the gun with Timothy and smoking pot with Poppy and River, but mostly I told her everything, and Gina just sat on the bed shaking her head and holding Angel like she was a precious, miraculous thing, which, I guess, she was.

The whole time I was telling Gina about what had happened, the phone beside the bed kept ringing. It rang probably two or three times, but she never answered it. Finally, when I was finished, I asked her, "How come the phone keeps ringing?"

"Well, I can't dance anymore," she said. "Or at least not for a long time." She nodded to a silver cane that leaned against the wall.

"Oh no," I said.

"Yeah, so I decided I would try being an independent escort for a while," she said.

"Oh," I said. "The classy date."

"That's right," she smiled. "It's only been a few days, but the phone has been ringing non-stop. I'm not booking anyone until late next week though, because I just need a little bit more time, but I think I'll be working a lot."

I nodded. "That's good, I guess."

She settled Angel in between two pillows and then gave me a super-hug which is a hug that crushes your spleen and almost squishes all your guts out. "I love you so much," she said. "I missed you like crazy."

"Me too," I said.

"I'm so sorry about your friend," she said, brushing some hair away from my face.

I looked over at Angel.

"We're going to get this all sorted out. Don't worry. We'll go see Meredith's brother tomorrow. First thing."

"Okay," I said.

"I have to let the group home know you're back. They've been calling every day since you guys took off. There were people out there *looking* for you, Tucker, did you know that?"

"No."

She sighed and ruffled my hair. "I'm going to run you a bubble bath," she said. "You stink."

While I was in the tub, Gina called Bright Light and fed Angel and ordered pizza for us. We ate on Gina's bed and watched a movie on TV about a goth man who had scissors for hands. After it was over, Gina fed Angel again and gave her a bath in the sink. Then she made a little nest for Angel on her bed out of pillows and blankets and told me it was time for me to get some sleep. I got into the bed across from hers, and she came over and pulled the covers up to my chin and tucked me in all tight and gave me a kiss on both cheeks and the forehead. And even though I'm eleven and way too old to be tucked in, I think that probably no matter how old you get, it is still one of the best feelings in the world to be tucked in by your mom.

\*\*\*

The next day we got some baby clothes and diapers for Angel and then took the bus to the Don Jail in Toronto. It took forever to get there, but Angel slept the whole time. On the bus, Gina told me about the dream she'd had while I was away. "It was awful, Tucker. One of the worst dreams I've ever had. One of those crazy ones where it's all so real that I think it's really happening. And it went on and on; it seemed to last a decade."

"What happened?" I said.

"Well, you were on this trip, and you kept taking rides from all these monsters."

"Monsters?"

"Horrible people. Like mass murderers and serial killers and rapists and psychopaths. And I was so worried for you. I was *so, so* worried because I knew they would hurt you. But the worst part was that there was nothing I could do about it. I wasn't there with you, I was just watching it all happen, you know, that kind of dream."

"Yeah."

"But they didn't hurt you. Every time, you just barely got away. I don't know how. It's like you had a force-field of protection around you."

"Huh," I said. I looked down at the bracelet that Poppy had given me and twisted it around my wrist.

"And *Elvis* was there. He wasn't a bad guy, he was just singing and playing guitar, but he was in the dream too. It was so weird."

I smiled, thinking of Relvis.

"Anyways, you're home safe with me now," she said. She squeezed my shoulder and gave me a little kiss on the head.

We didn't talk too much for the rest of the way there but I thought a lot about everything.

\*\*\*

When we got to the prison, we had to be searched before we could see Steve, and the guard took Gina's nail file and my Swiss Army knife away and said we could have them back when we left. We were shown to a little cubicle with a plate of glass, two chairs, and a phone. I sat in the chair next to the phone and Gina sat in the other one and held Angel on her lap. On the other side of the glass, a guard brought Steve in. Steve wore an orange jumpsuit and his hair was black and shaggy and fell to his chin. He sat down in the chair across from me and looked into my eyes. They were the same green beach-glass eyes as Meredith's, and it hurt me to look at them because I knew that I would never look in her eyes again. Steve's hands were handcuffed together, but he picked up the phone.

I picked up the phone.

He raised his eyebrows.

"Hi," I said.

"Hi," he said. "Do I know you?"

"My name is Tucker Malone. Meredith was my best friend. She died giving birth the day before yesterday in Los Angeles, California. This is her baby."

Steve looked over at Angel and his green eyes got soft and watery. He blinked hard a few times and sniffed and rubbed his face. "What's her name?"

"Angel," I said.

He smiled at the baby. I could tell by the way his face crumpled up that he already loved her. "She's so small," he said.

"She's premature," I said.

He nodded and wiped his eyes again.

"Meredith said to bring her to you. She said you would know what to do."

He looked up to the ceiling and half-laughed. Then he stared at the baby for a while. She made gurbally sounds and Steve smiled big at her. "Don't tell me you're the father," he said, turning to me.

"No," I said. "Uh-uh." I could feel my face get hot.

Gina shook her head.

"Who is?"

"I ... I don't know," I said.

"Did Meredith know?"

"I'm not sure," I said. "She never said anything about him."

What good would it do for Steve to know that Angel's father was a rapist? It wouldn't help Angel. It wouldn't help anything. It was the kind of lie I felt okay about telling. Maybe Angel would never have to find out.

Steve was getting out of prison in twenty-eight days. He had a girlfriend named Kim who lived in Niagara Falls and he told us to take the baby to Kim tomorrow after he'd had a chance to talk to her. Kim would look after the baby until he got out and then they would raise her together.

"She's been wanting a baby for a while now anyways," he said. "Guess she got her wish." He gave us Kim's address and phone number and Gina wrote it all down on the back of an old receipt. "She works nights so she'll be home all day," he said.

"Okay," I said. "Steve?"

"Yeah?"

"Do you think it would be okay if I came to visit Angel sometimes. Just to see how she's doing?"

"Sure, kid. You can babysit for us every weekend if you want." He smiled at Gina and winked at her.

"And Kim won't mind?"

"She'll be ecstatic," he said.

"Steve?"

"Yeah, Tucker?"

"Do you think it would be okay if I kept Meredith's Walkman? And some of her tapes?"

Steve bit his bottom lip and nodded. "I think she would want you to have them," he said.

Then I passed the phone to Gina because my throat closed up with sadness and I couldn't talk anymore. Gina told Steve she would leave our phone number at the front desk for him in case he needed to get a hold of us. She asked him if there was anything else we could do, anyone else we should call.

"I'll take care of it," Steve said. He thanked us for coming and for looking after Angel.

I took the phone back from Gina. "She was saving up money for you," I said. "To bail you out. She had a lot saved. I'm not sure how much. I don't know where it is. Probably at Bright Light. The group home. I don't think she put it in the bank."

"Thanks for telling me," Steve said.

"So, I guess I'll see you next month then," I said.

"See ya on the outside, kid." He nodded once, then Steve hung up his phone and I hung up mine and the guard came and led him away.

# 32

On the bus ride home, I said to Gina, "So now you have to tell me about my father. Once and for all."

"Now?"

"Right now," I said.

"Are you sure?"

"Positive."

"You don't want to wait until we get home?"

"No."

She took a big sigh. She looked out the window for a second, then looked back at me. "Your father's name was Mark Baxter," she said. "He was a bartender at the pub I worked at in Paris when I was a teenager."

"Was he your boyfriend?"

"No."

"Did you want him to be your boyfriend?"

"No. He was thirty-six years old."

"He was almost twenty years older than you?"

"And he was married."

"Oh," I said. "So ... "

"So one night, he had been drinking during his shift, and he came up behind me while I was stocking the beer cooler and he ... he raped me."

"Oh." I looked down at my hands. A giant had just punched me in the stomach.

"I'm sorry, Tucker. That's why I never wanted to tell you. I didn't want you to have to live with that."

"Did you tell anybody?"

"I told my mom. She didn't believe me. She said I must have

seduced him, gotten him drunk and seduced him, she said. She thought my skirts were too short and my tops were too tight. She didn't believe me. Or she was ashamed of me. I don't know." She shrugged.

"Did he know about me?"

Gina nodded.

"But, he ... "

She shook her head. "He denied that you were his. He said that I'd slept with half of Paris and there was no way. But it wasn't true. He begged me not to tell his wife."

"Did you?"

"No. I made him pay me five thousand dollars not to tell her. And I used the money to move away, right after I had you."

"In the laundromat?"

"In the laundromat," she smiled, nodding.

"Do you have a picture of him?"

"No."

"Did he ever ask about me? Does he know who I am?"

"I never saw him again after I left."

"You never talked to him either?"

"No."

"But—"

"He's a bad person, Tucker. I don't want him around you. Ever."

"So, that means that ... half of me is a bad person too."

"No, honey. Don't say that. That's not true. You're a good person. You're the best person I know." Gina wiped away a tear that had sneaked out the corner of her eye.

"I'm sorry," I said.

"You don't have to be sorry, Tucker. You didn't do anything wrong, okay? This was *not* your fault."

"I know, but I'm sorry that it happened to you."

"Well, I got you out of it," she said. "So I guess it was the worst thing *and* the best thing that ever happened to me."

I leaned into her and closed my eyes. She put her arm around me and kissed me on top of the head. We were quiet for the rest of the way back to Niagara Falls and I thought about how the world is full of terrible things, and really great stuff too, and you just never know what you're going to get, but it will be some combination of both. Every donut has its hole.

As we got off the bus in front of the Niagara Motel, I held Angel against my chest and watched as Gina gripped her cane and struggled to get down the steps. She was not the same woman she had been when we first got off the bus in Niagara Falls, and, I guess, I wasn't the same boy either.

# TUCKER'S MIX-TAPE

(to remember my trip to Los Angeles, California, April 25 to May 1, 1992)

1. "Cheeseburger in Paradise," Jimmy Buffet
2. "Smells Like Teen Spirit," Nirvana
3. Cheers Theme Song ("Where Everybody Knows Your Name"), Gary Portnoy
4. "Hit the Road Jack," Ray Charles
5. "California Dreamin'," The Mamas & The Papas
6. "Stand by Me," Ben E. King
7. "People Are Strange," The Doors
8. "Heart of Gold," Neil Young
9. "Come as You Are," Nirvana
10. "Mustang Sally," Muddy Waters
11. "In the Ghetto," Elvis
12. "Folsom Prison Blues," Johnny Cash
13. "I've Been Everywhere," Johnny Cash
14. "Six Days on the Road," Dave Dudley
15. "Black or White," Michael Jackson
16. "It's the End of the World as We Know It (And I Feel Fine)," R.E.M.
17. "Been Caught Stealing," Jane's Addiction
18. "Whiter Shade of Pale," Procol Harum
19. "Boys Don't Cry," The Cure
20. "Ain't No Sunshine," Bill Withers
21. "Bird on a Wire," Kate Wolf
22. "I'll Fly Away," Hank Williams

# ACKNOWLEDGMENTS

THANK YOU:

John Little for being my favourite dad; Jennifer Little for medical and preemie baby info, sending Niagara Falls postcards and tourist info, and being my mom; Ben Burgis for tips on what eleven-year-old boys would/would not say/do; Trevor Hagerman for trucking info; Mary Little for sending Niagara Falls photos; Ron Twigg for help with fact checking; Tamsin Pukonen; Timothy Goldman for sending his video footage of the L.A. Riots; Alfred Lomas and L.A. Gang Tours for showing me Compton, Watts, and South Central L.A.; Jane Doe for graciously agreeing to let me interview her about escorting; Kevin Chong and *Joyland* for publishing "Niagara Motel" (the story); the University of British Columbia Okanagan and the BC Arts Council for financial support during the research and creation of this novel; Anne Fleming, my first reader and a true believer in Tucker's world; Nancy Holmes, Matt Rader, for feedback and guidance; Alexandra Writers' Centre Society and Loft 112 for hosting me in Calgary as 2014 Writer in Residence; Terri Jean Bedford, Amy Lebovitch, and Valerie Scott for fighting the good fight; Willy Vlautin; my agent, Hilary McMahon; my publisher, Brian Lam; my editor, Susan Safyan, and the whole team at Arsenal; special thank you to Warren Sookocheff, without whom there would be no Gina.

ASHLEY LITTLE'S *Anatomy of a Girl Gang* won the Ethel Wilson Fiction Prize (BC Book Prizes), was shortlisted for the Vancouver Book Award and longlisted for the IMPAC Dublin Literary Award, and has been translated into Croatian and Italian. Her young adult novel *The New Normal* (Orca Book Publishers) won the Sheila A. Egoff Children's Literature Prize. Ashley's first novel, *Prick: Confessions of a Tattoo Artist* (Tightrope Books) was a finalist for a ReLit award and has been optioned for film. She has an MFA from the University of British Columbia. She lives in the Okanagan Valley.

*ashleylittle.com*